The BFF Role

Jaysee Jewel

THE BFF ROLE

Copyright © 2023 by Jaysee Jewel

All rights reserved.

Book cover designs by Victoria Chevalier

Edited by Melissa Cole

Names: Jewel, Jaysee.

Title: The BFF Role / Jaysee Jewel.

Subjects: Young Adult / Romance

First Edition: August 2023

ISBN: 979-8-9872796-3-2

https://jayseejewel.mystrikingly.com/

For Xiang,

You were right about me.

Introduction

I was seventeen when I realized I was living inside a romance novel.

Two days later, I also realized I wasn't the main character.

I didn't take offense to either of these facts, of course. I should have expected it as soon as I became aware of who was pretty and who was not, as well as who was charismatic and who was lacking in social graces. I was ranked on the lower end of each scale, though not the lowest. Man, this makes me sound superficial, but it's just reality, especially for a teenager.

I'll start from the beginning, since it might give you a better understanding of how I discovered the whole "living in a book" thing. Hopefully it'll make me look less crazy too.

First of all, my name is Zilla—don't question the name. It's just a childhood nickname that stuck—and as I said, I was never particularly pretty or likeable, even from a young age. I have straight black hair from a weird mixture of Asian and Irish genes, matching dark eyes, and an average body with no curves. I'm not ugly or plain—just normal. If I was either of those two extremes, I might have still had the potential to be the main character. Main characters are either *very* pretty or *so* plain it stands out. One creates a standard to look up to and the other makes a lead character relatable to its readers. As I said, I was neither.

I don't judge people in real life based on appearances. It's only in the context of my *book* theory. Well, most of the time. Sure, I can be superficial sometimes, but at least I'm aware of it, right? That makes it okay.... Okay, not really, but maybe when I stop being a teenager I'll become less shallow.

In terms of personality, I'm not particularly quiet or loud either. That's another trait that kept me out of the MC territory. I liked dinosaurs growing up, especially the stegosaurus, then I transitioned into horses at the age of ten before slowly drifting right past crushes on boys and into medicine. Becoming a nurse became my unenthusiastic life goal and turning into a doctor was a vague wish. However, I'm not particularly passionate about either route. It was just the path that felt right and convenient while filling out those high school questionnaires about the future.

Main characters generally don't have such specifically boring dreams. They don't think "I want to be a nurse because it's stable and would make my parents happy". They're always obsessed with something creative or quirky to the point of being annoying to readers. The wannabe artist in the book always becomes a famous architect by twenty-five. The girl obsessed with writing eventually becomes a world-famous journalist at twenty-eight. The college athlete wins the world championship. You know what I mean. There is no main character who wants to become a nurse and then just does it. If there is, it isn't common in the books I read.

Speaking of books, I'm not an avid reader, but I've seen enough rom-coms and read enough novels to know all the romance tropes. MCs often love writing or drawing or music, and something is always holding them back from their creative aspirations. Maybe it's their insecurities, a rival, or strict parents who push their own unattained dreams onto their children.

Either the main character has some unrealistic artistic goal *or* they're an interior designer just starting out in their career, somehow managing to live in a huge, fancy apartment despite the job probably not bringing in a ton of money.

Nurses, on the other hand, are boring and not very glamorous or artsy. Have you ever heard of a girl getting swept off her feet by a handsome young man while cleaning up someone else's vomit? Not super romantic. I'm not hating on nurses, of course. I want to be one. But again, that's not a typical book character's goal in life. Thus, I couldn't be the main character.

Now, I know what you're thinking: *not only is she superficial and harsh but she hates nurses too.* And you'd be partly right. But I'm a teenager. Cut me some slack. Or don't. I'll grow out of it, hopefully, for my own sake and the sake of the *real* main character in my life. But I'm getting ahead of myself.

So, everything I just said explains why I'm not the lead character in this book world. But who is? That's easy.

My best friend, Cindy, is everything you would want in a relatable main character. She fulfils every girl's dream. She's simple enough for the readers to put themselves in her shoes, but not bland enough to be boring.

Cindy checkmarks every box without even trying. When we first met in kindergarten, she was very plain and didn't stand out. (Not that I care about such things. It's just something I often see mentioned in books. I'm calling out the clichés.) She had brown hair that she despised for being curly, though I thought it was quite cute. She also had those chocolate brown eyes, so different from mine, which are practically black, and they would shine brightly whenever she talked about something she loved. (Again, I don't hate *my* eyes. I'm just comparing for explanation's sake.) She was sweet, honest, and went to church regularly with her parents. She was a great friend and just an overall wonderful person, but as much as I loved her, she wasn't anything beyond plain to objective eyes.

However, when we turned seventeen, I noticed some changes happening in her. Insecure Cindy was finally reaching an overdue growth spurt and filling out nicely. Good for her.

That was the first sign. A lot of romance movies start with the girl blossoming overnight or during summer break. But such a thing happening isn't out of the ordinary in reality, so I didn't pay it any mind.

Then, just as her changes started happening, a new boy moved into our small town and created quite a stir. Our class consisted of only 100 students, so everybody knew everyone else, even if they didn't want to. Small towns in Illinois tend to be that way.

Derek shared some of our classes and I eventually began to hear from other girls that he was becoming a little famous for his good looks. He was cute in the boy-next-door kind of way.

His name was Derek Daniels. He had dark brown hair, dimples, green eyes, and a strong build (but not in a jock way). If I wasn't so focused on my own goals and hanging out with my best friend Cindy—who I adore by the way—I might have had a crush on him. But then I saw Cindy blush while staring at him and immediately knew he was off-limits. Rule number one of having a best friend: don't intentionally chase a boy when your best friend is already interested in him. No problem. I didn't plan to date anyone until I was safely graduated and in college anyway.

Big deal, you're thinking. *So, Cindy has a crush on this new boy. People have crushes all the time. It's high school! Sounds like you're overthinking things.*

Yes. I agree. Crushes and growth spurts are perfectly normal.

But then things started happening that were *really* out of the ordinary.

First, Cindy and this new boy bumped into each other in the hallway. Okay. Fine.

But their books went flying, one of them hitting me in the face, and then they fell right on top of each other in that "she's on top of him and their lips are a centimeter apart and they may have had an accidental kiss" way. Once the blushing and apologizing and nervous giggling ended, I helped Cindy to her feet and started picking up her books. By the time I had them all in hand, Derek was running off with a red face and she was completely frozen.

Very awkward for me.

"That was super weird," I whispered with a laugh. She wasn't laughing, though. She was turning pink, her mouth agape, and her hands were hovering in front of her as though she was still on the floor, reliving falling on top of him. She was lovestruck; because of course she was.

A week later—amidst the two constantly sneaking glances at each other in class, then looking away when they got caught rather than acting normal and initiating the conversation they clearly wanted to start—they were both assigned to cleaning duty, which consisted of washing the blackboards and sweeping the floor to learn responsibility. I had planned to head straight home after class and leave them to it, but I forgot one of my algebra books on my desk, so when I popped back into the classroom to grab it, I witnessed Cindy accidentally covering Derek in dust from the chalkboard eraser. She was profusely apologizing while waving the eraser around, sending more dust into the already toxic air. She must have accidentally hit him somehow and sent the dust into his face. Very cliché. Why did we even use chalkboards nowadays anyway? Most schools at least had a whiteboard or projector.

Whatever. I rolled my eyes, grabbed my book, and left. I may have also smirked as I walked away, amused at the ridiculousness of the situation and relieved I wasn't involved. Plus, it was nice to see my best friend talking to her crush.

But the shenanigans didn't stop there. That was just the beginning.

That weekend, Cindy and I went to a restaurant and she ran into Derek on the way to the bathroom—*literally* ran into him. She spilled soup all over his shirt. Why was she carrying soup to the bathroom, you ask? She'd forgotten she was holding it, supposedly. How? I have no clue. Cindy was prone to zoning out, particularly when thinking about Derek, but it still felt suspicious...as in "terrible levels of writing" ridiculous.

The next time it happened, it was actually my fault. I convinced Cindy to talk to Derek on Friday, since a whole week of seeing them eye each other like sad puppies became downright frustrating. Plus, I wanted to help her out. Cindy was the type who needed encouragement every now and then. However, while she was approaching him in the school hallway, she slipped on nothing and fell into his arms AGAIN! Swooning ensued and I was lucky she didn't faint.

Gym class? She hit him right in the face during dodgeball and had to lead him to the infirmary.

Science class? Derek and Cindy were paired up and their beaker exploded even though we weren't supposed to be using it.

Cafeteria? Cindy spilled her drink on him and accidentally started a food fight. I ducked out of the room for that one. I heard later that all the people involved had to clean it up.

Weird, right? Food fights aren't normal. They only happen in books and movies, to my knowledge. It was the first and last food fight to happen in our school. More evidence for my theory.

That food fight fiasco was my true confirmation. If it was just one or two coincidences, fine. But this many? Something was up.

And it couldn't be a coincidence that I was the perfect best friend who was always supportive of Cindy but had my own life so it wouldn't interfere with hers. I fit the role of the cliché best friend perfectly. You know what type of character I'm talking about—the girl or boy who wears glasses and only speaks in sarcasm and dresses in strange clothes without feeling embarrassed by it. I fit the first two, sort of, and my clothes weren't weird but weren't exactly trendy either.

So, that was when everything fell into place. Something had always felt off about this whole high school experience—we had way too many field trips, everyone was either really attractive or not attractive at all, and the breaks between classes were longer than those in neighboring high schools—so *this* was the only explanation. We were in a book. Cindy was the female lead. Derek was the male lead.

And I was the best friend—the side character.

It took a few days for me to come to terms with this reality. After all, who wants to be the ignored best friend no one really cares about? Everyone wants to be the main character, right?

But, after giving it a little thought, I realized this was perfect for me. Now that I understood the clichés, I could study a few romance paperbacks and watch a few romantic comedies. Then I'd be able to predict every single dangerous coincidence coming Cindy's way and I could help her avoid them. I might have been generally unconcerned when it came to the majority of people's well-being, but when it came to Cindy, I'd do almost anything to help her.

This knowledge would also help me shove my best friend into the main romance plot. That was the BFF's role, right? To help the friend get with the boy she likes? More importantly, once the couple fell in love, the best friend rarely had to take part in the drama except to offer advice when the couple had a fight. I'd finally be able to relax and live my life without worrying about sudden kidnappings or scandals or whatever random events happened in romance movies. I wouldn't have to worry about Cindy conveniently tripping over her feet either. It always gave me a near heart attack hearing her scream when she did.

I was honestly relieved after I came to terms with this reality. Being in a book made life predictable, and predictability could take away a lot of anxiety.

Well, there was one issue. If we ended up being in a mixed genre romance, like a romance thriller, I might end up dying tragically so the author could create a new, traumatizing arc for Cindy. But if that was the case, there'd be no way around it, so there was no point worrying about that aspect.

So, murder aside, everything was set to go swimmingly.

That brings us to the present day. I am eighteen years old, a senior in high school, and the mid-year prom is coming up. I am completely self-aware, have accepted my given role, and am ready to help my ditzy friend with her love life.

Prom was the perfect opportunity to finally get Cindy past the story's introduction and into the actual plot. Plus, despite my studious habits, I loved dress shopping, and the makeover scenes were always my favorite part of a movie. So, it was time to kick my fairy godmother plans into gear, find her a gorgeous dress, and send her flying into Derek's arms.

My only real fear was being roped into the whole "the side character also needs to fall in love so the ending is wrapped up nicely" trope. I didn't want to fall prey to all those annoying coincidences too. That was why I needed to get Cindy and Derek together as fast as I could so there would be no danger to me. Then I could just fade into the background.

That should be easy. Nothing could possibly go wrong!

PART ONE

Chapter 1

"He did what?!" I hissed, ready to throw my cafeteria fork in rage as Cindy's blushing face nearly disappeared under her food tray. We were seated across from each other at a small table in the cafeteria. Cindy had just updated me on the boy I'd been hoping would ask her to prom, Derek Daniels.

"How do you 'accidentally' ask someone to prom?" I continued, not caring how loud I was since the hum of the surrounding conversations overpowered my voice. "That doesn't even make sense."

"I doubt it was an accident," Cindy said feebly, fiddling with her own fork. "He probably likes her. She *is* the most popular girl in school, after all, and—"

"He's a moron if he thinks *Samantha Stanford* is a good catch. She only dates guys with open wallets, then dumps them once she wrings them dry. I thought Derek was smarter than that." Normally I wasn't so harsh with other girls, but I made an exception for Samantha.

Cindy peeked at me. "You shouldn't talk about her that way."

She was right but stereotyping people had become a habit, mainly when I was in "book best friend" mode, as I sometimes called it.

"I didn't expect you to be so angry about this," Cindy continued meekly.

Of course I was angry! This was screwing up my whole plan for a peaceful end of senior year. Prom was supposed to be their first date! Now Derek had ruined it by accidentally asking the ever-so-popular (and mean) Samantha Stanford to prom instead of Cindy. Samantha once tried to copy off my test in the sixth grade and when I told the teacher, she lied and said I was cheating instead. The teacher believed her over me.

"I'm angry *for* you," I explained quickly, slouching down in my chair. I shouldn't get worked up. This could still lead to some drama that would eventually result in a happy ending. "I know you've liked him since he transferred here last semester and it's clear he likes you too! I'm just trying to figure out why he'd ask someone else out when you're clearly the ideal girl for him."

"I don't think that's true…" Her voice trailed off and she stared at the mushy peas in her tray, avoiding eye contact. She never stood up for herself or believed any man could like her—typical main character mentality and typical Cindy too. She was too much of a sweetheart to think badly of Samantha or Derek or anyone. She also believed everyone else was better than her, including me and Samantha. I, myself, knew that wasn't true and told her so as often as I could. She never believed me, though.

"He likes you, Cindy. Do not give up." I resisted the urge to roll my eyes and looked across the cafeteria at Derek instead. He was sitting next to mean-girl Samantha and her other popular friends. He looked uncomfortable and desperate to return to his group of geeky, video game obsessed buddies at the other end of the cafeteria. What a mess he'd gotten himself into. I didn't feel the least bit sorry for him.

This "accidental prom date" was obviously just a cheap tactic the author was using to create drama and jealousy. I was confident Cindy would overcome this trial as all protagonists did, but it was my job to help her accomplish that.

"You know, you don't *need* a boy to ask you to prom," I said. "We can just go together. We could invite Tammy and Leandri too. I don't think their boyfriends are coming." Our two other friends lived in the next town over. We got to know each other during summer camp. They'd be perfect for the dramatic scene where the group of girls enter the prom in slow motion wearing fancy dresses and looking hot while rock music plays in the background.

"Sure," Cindy said, completely noncommittal. She was already looking longingly at Derek, turning away every so often when their eyes met. I just shook my head in disgust and stabbed at my food, trying to figure out where this plot would go. Would me escorting her be enough to keep things moving, or was there something else about to occur that I hadn't predicted?

Aha! That was it. Cindy being jealous on her own wasn't enough. I needed to make Derek feel it too. I had to make him jealous somehow. I needed to get him to say: "I never wanted to go out with Samantha! I wanted to go with you and was just too shy/stupid to tell you." I had no clue how to make him jealous, though, other than giving Cindy a makeover, which wasn't my area of expertise. Nursing didn't offer a lot of hair and makeup experience.

Unfortunately, the author was way ahead of me. She had a solution planned to solve my problem, and it was something I would have immediately shot down if I'd had any say.

The answer to my problems came in the form of Axel Burns, the most handsome, charismatic, and scandalous playboy in our grade. I had never expected him to come into Cindy's life since he was everything she wasn't, but unfortunately, that was probably the exact reason the author chose him.

Chapter 2

The next morning, I missed my first two classes because I had a dentist appointment. Then they discovered two cavities and I missed my third class too, which was a real shame because it was right at that moment that the author's intervention in Cindy's life occurred. I couldn't believe I missed it!

But I'm getting ahead of myself.

When I entered my fourth class, English, and sat next to Cindy, I found her pale and panicked. Her hands were flat on the table, her book bag was unopened, and she wasn't even looking at Derek as the teacher chatted about Julius Caesar. None of the other students seemed to notice her plight, other than maybe Derek, who looked her way once before turning back to the front of the classroom.

Ten minutes in, I passed Cindy a note asking what was wrong, because of course I did. I was the caring best friend, both in the book and in reality.

AXEL BURNS ASKED ME TO PROM, was her reply.

I was sure I had the stereotypical shocked look on my face, and it probably looked exceedingly comical.

Axel Burns. He was a well-known guy who bore both moderate intelligence and devilish good looks. He had blond hair that grew just a little past his ears and it was only sometimes purposefully styled. He had steel blue eyes that I was sure were said to "sparkle" in the book's description of him, a toned and muscular body, though it was only to the point where it made his jawline and cheeks have the right shape, and tons of natural swagger that drew everyone to him. (Do people even say swagger anymore? I'm not hip enough to know.)

All the girls loved him...except Cindy, of course...and me...and probably half of the girls in class, honestly. The saying "all the girls loved him" was just what people wrote in books. He *was* popular, though, and always surrounded by the popular kids, including Samantha Stanford. He also *got* with a lot of them, in the "took what he wanted from them, then dumped them when he got bored" way, according to the grapevine. Rumor said he'd never dated a girl longer than two months, though who knew how accurate that was? He was basically the male version of Samantha and just as attractive. I was sure he was rich too, though I never cared enough to investigate.

I should have known Axel would get involved as soon as prom month rolled around. He was the obvious love rival. He fit the bill to a T. I should have realized it earlier. He fit every standard for a love rival who would pursue the girl but never get her in the end. How often did you see a blond male lead actually *get* the girl? It was rare...at least in the films I watched. The main reason I got so upset when Cindy told me about Axel was because I didn't want to see her get hurt, and he would definitely hurt her somehow. I just knew he'd cheat right away.

It wasn't surprising that the author finally decided to let Axel interfere. Cindy's story hadn't had any tragedy yet, so heartbreak was bound to come along at some point. Maybe she'd date Axel for a bit while Derek dated Samantha, then midway through college they would both get dumped or cheated on and realize the other person was right for them all along.

But that was such a waste of time! I couldn't wait that long! As the best friend, it should be my job to warn Cindy about boys like that and help her avoid them from the get-go. There had to be a better, faster way to create drama.

"He didn't," I hissed, shoving the note about Axel back at Cindy and accidentally drawing everyone's attention for a moment.

"Miss Yahui," our teacher said, spinning around with a frown. "Is there something you'd like to share with the class about this topic?" He pointed at the board where the word FOILS was written with examples listed underneath.

"Only that evil characters shouldn't associate with nice, sweet, innocent characters," I said quietly. I didn't care about getting an A in this class. It didn't have much to do with medicine, so there was no harm in giving a dumb answer to the question.

"I don't think you understand the role a foil is supposed to play," Mr. Douglas said, looking disappointed in me. "Perhaps you should review the pages we just read *five minutes ago*." He pointedly looked at the unopened textbook on my desk and I flipped to the correct page without skipping a beat.

I didn't mind the teacher's sarcasm. He was just doing his job and I wasn't making it easy for him. "Sorry, sir."

When the teacher finally refocused on his lesson, I turned back to Cindy with wide eyes and mouthed the word NO to her. She was not going to prom with Axel Burns! As her overprotective friend, I wouldn't allow it.

But Cindy didn't look as terrified of Axel as I thought. Rather, she looked nervously excited. That pale jitteriness I'd noticed earlier wasn't from a fear of the unknown. It was from the thrill of a popular boy asking her out.

Oh no! Was Cindy prone to the "I can fix him" trope? Not good! She couldn't fall for the cheating playboy when the stereotypical lead was sitting right in front of her! Derek might be an idiot, but at least he wasn't bad news.

I had to put a stop to this.

Chapter 3

"So," I said to the sparkly, handsome Axel as he sat down next to a nervous Cindy and draped his arm around her. We were at our corner lunch table again and I was across from them with my arms crossed and food untouched. Axel had dragged a chair over to join us and it made the once cozy area feel cramped. "How did you two meet, Axel? I've never even seen you speak to Cindy before."

Axel was handsome in that "he gets all the girls but he'll never fall in love with you" kind of way. He wasn't cute like the boy-next-door, Golden Retriever Derek. Derek looked harmless and thoughtful while Axel looked manipulative and selfish, like a cat. I knew Cindy only said yes to his invitation because she wasn't used to the attention he was giving her.

Noting my obvious dislike from my crossed arms and raised eyebrows, Axel shot me a lady-killer smile—perfectly white and with straight teeth included—and tightened his grip on my friend's shoulder. "She helped me pick up my books when I dropped them in the hallway and it was love at first sight," he said carelessly, like it didn't matter how or why they met.

Right. More convenient falls in the hallway. Just like what happened with Derek.

The funny thing was, I totally believed him. That was probably exactly what happened. Perhaps the author only knew one way to introduce new characters.

"That's so sweet," I lied, mirroring his fake smile. "What did you like about her?"

"Zilla…" Cindy started to interject meekly, but I stuck to my guns. This Axel needed at least *some* resistance. Hopefully he'd be out of the picture by the end of prom, when Derek confessed his true feelings, but I still hated the situation regardless. It was too risky.

"Don't worry about me," Axel said to Cindy, smiling down at her. He was a foot taller than her, since she was so short, and she seemed to adore the difference.

"What I *will* say, Cindy's best friend," Axel continued, "is I love Cindy because she's adorably cute, super sweet, and completely selfless."

"Of course she is." I agreed completely. I knew he didn't mean it, though. He barely knew her. "And what do *you* bring to the table?" I tapped my boot on the floor. My dark clothes felt appropriate, not only because they countered the bright pinks of Cindy's outfit and the sky blues of Axel's, but because I was the one in charge here. I would lead the conversation—not Axel.

"Whoa." Axel raised his arms defensively. "We just met yesterday. There's no need to interview me. It's not like we're getting married."

"Oh, I'm *so* sorry." I already knew he had no good qualities to speak of. Well, that was a little harsh, but in this book world, he was a villain. Villains didn't have good qualities. "You're right. It's not like you two are going to date."

He raised an eyebrow but didn't respond to that part. "If you don't have a date yet, I have a good buddy who would be happy to go with you to prom," he said, clearly trying to butter me up. "If you want, I can hook you up. Do you want his number?"

"Oh." I tilted my head and smiled, like he'd just done me the biggest favor ever. "That's so thoughtful. Thank you so much." He was so obnoxious.

Axel just smiled at me, probably thinking his façade had me totally fooled.

Unbelievable.

If he wasn't gone by the time prom ended, I'd dig up some dirt on him and *make* Cindy dump him. He needed to be humbled anyway. Rejection from a girl like her might bring him down a peg or two.

Chapter 4

S hopping for prom dresses was super fun, but most of it consisted of me trying to remind Cindy about her feelings for Derek, as well as dredging up negative rumors about Axel. I barely had to dig to find them. He didn't exactly have a stellar reputation. However, my constant gossip seemed to backfire, and Cindy took it upon herself to defend Axel from my 'unfair' rampage.

"You're being too hard on him," she said quietly as she exited the changing room wearing a fitted yellow dress that was too tight for her and made her look like a banana. "You've always been the one to say that rumors should be ignored and we should judge people only after we've met them."

"Yes, well, I've met him now and have confirmed that all the rumors are true," I fibbed from my leather chair outside the changing rooms. We were in a thrift store since neither of us had the money to buy pricey dresses and didn't care about fashion anyway. "Not that one. Try the green one. No! Wait. Try the blue. I think that one suits you more." I had already told her I thought the pink dress fit best, but she kept saying it wasn't "mature" enough to match Axel's vibe. In my opinion, his blue eyes and her pink dress complemented each other, but I didn't think that was what she wanted to hear.

"You barely gave him a chance to say anything," Cindy continued, stepping back behind the curtain and kicking the dress off.

"But you don't seriously like him, do you?" I asked nervously.

There was a long pause, then the sound of a zipper getting caught. "Can you help me, Zilla? I'm stuck."

"You're avoiding the question," I said as I stepped inside. I helped her zip up the blue dress, then stepped back to examine it. The cut was too low. It would fall off if she stood at...well, any angle. "Let's try the green one. And what about Derek? I thought you liked him." Or rather, I *knew* she liked him.

She blushed, of course, and as she slipped the dress sleeve off her shoulder, she spoke so quietly I nearly missed what she said. "He doesn't like me."

But I did hear her, thank goodness. "I have seen him looking at you every day in class. If he doesn't like you, I'll eat my hat." Saying silly lines like that didn't suit me, but I was in a romance novel, so cheesy quotes were allowed.

"You don't even wear hats," Cindy muttered as she slipped into the green dress. It wasn't the best, but it fit better than the others and the forest green looked pretty nice. I still preferred the pink but this was her decision so I wouldn't say more.

"This one looks good, *and* if I'm proven wrong about Axel, I'll buy a hat and eat it right in front of you." I would never be caught dead doing such a thing, of course, but it made her laugh so that was enough. Cindy was like a little sister to me, and a sometimes depressed one at that, so any smile was a triumph.

However, despite doing a cute makeover an hour before the event and admiring the alterations her mother had made to improve the dress, I still became overwhelmed with dread as the prom date arrived. I was beginning to fear this book we were trapped inside wasn't actually a sweet, wholesome romance. It might be a horror, or at the very least, a thriller. What if Axel was secretly a serial killer? The thought horrified me. The only positive about that was that Cindy's character type was usually the last to survive. She fit the final girl trope perfectly...though that meant *I* would likely be the first one to die.

Stop thinking about thrillers, Zilla. Just focus on prom and making it as awesome as possible for Cindy. If Axel was a serial killer, I would stop him somehow. The more likely thing he'd end up being was a cheating playboy, and I'd stop him then, too.

Chapter 5

As I joined Axel's best friend Timothy Williams on the front steps of the school after being dropped off by my father, I watched that obnoxiously handsome jerk Axel lead Cindy into the crowded, hot, and ridiculously loud gymnasium where the prom was taking place. The whole school now smelled of strong perfume and sweat, and the air was filled with blaring music and shouts from students making their song requests.

The tense, night time setting and its contrast with Axel's good looks caused my worries about thrillers to resurface. What if this was a crime story about a sweet, innocent girl who was lured in by a hot serial killer? It was like Ted Bundy, but if the villain was actually good looking.

That, or this was still a romance but also a tragedy. Cindy would spend most of her life married to Axel, who cheated on her constantly, then in her thirties she would finally wise up, break up with the scoundrel, and rediscover her spark for her childhood crush.

What a huge hassle that would be for both her and me.

As my date and I waltzed into the crowded gym and the kids around us started dancing to mainstream pop music, I kept an eye on my best friend. I also sent frequent glances toward both Derek and Axel. The Timothy boy who escorted me in tried to drag me into the mass of sparkly bodies to dance, but I didn't let it interfere with my mission. I had to ensure Axel was in my sights at all times.

Thankfully, both of the foolish but sweet protagonists were stiffly dancing with their hot partners and looking extremely uncomfortable. Derek was wrapped up in Samantha's arms like a hamster squeezed by a child and Cindy was managing to dance with Axel while staying as drawn away from him as possible. I didn't miss the cliché glances the two leads were exchanging, ignoring their partners as they undoubtedly imagined dancing with the person they *really* liked. I could tell Samantha wasn't happy that her date kept looking away, but every time Cindy glanced at Derek, Axel would smirk and pull her closer. There were a few times when this nearly made them kiss. He was clearly having fun messing with her. He must be the type who enjoyed a challenge. It was a bit gross.

"Not a fan of dancing?" Timothy asked me when I accidentally stepped on his foot while dancing. He was lucky I wasn't wearing heels. "Or just nervous because we barely know each other?"

"No. Neither," I said, distracted. I kept an eye on Axel and nearly gasped when he leaned toward Cindy, closer and longer this time. Was he going to kiss her for real?

Timothy followed my gaze and laughed. "I see how it is. You're into Axel."

"Oh, come on. That's your conclusion?" I sighed and turned back to this boy I'd just met. He was cute in a chiseled, rugged way and I understood why he hung out with the popular kids. Unfortunately for him, he was just a side character like me. He was only here to fill in the blanks. "I'm keeping an eye on my best friend because she's..." I trailed off as I turned back to Axel and Cindy. Cindy had just pushed him away, rejecting his blatant attempt at a kiss, and was swiftly shoving her way through the crowd to one of the exiting hallways.

"Oh no," I said, then added, "Actually, this is great." I pulled away from a protesting Timothy as I watched her head into one of the halls where I was sure she'd dramatically cry on the floor and rethink her life. It only took Axel thirty minutes to ruin prom for her. That had to be a new record.

I looked at Derek. Had he seen it? He had! He was already detangling himself from Samantha and heading after Cindy. That meant I *shouldn't* go to comfort her. That was *his* job now!

"Hey, Zilla, it's pretty rude to ignore your date," Timothy said, catching up with me and grabbing my arm lightly. "Could you—"

"Samantha Stanford's going to need a new dance partner in a second," I said, nodding toward the gorgeous girl in her sparkly gold dress. She was currently huffing and trying to prevent Derek from leaving, but sure enough, a moment later, Derek completely broke off from the dance and headed after Cindy. Finally!

Grinning, I turned back to Timothy. "See? I know you're interested in Sam, not me. No need to hide it."

Timothy gave me a funny look, which I deserved, I suppose. I had no reason to believe he liked Samantha. I had just assumed lots of guys in our grade would date her if they could. But it worked out, since he shrugged, thanked me, and headed off to sweep the preppy girl off her feet. I wished him luck in my head, relieved I'd been right, then slowly headed to the edge of the room to get a peek down that hallway. I was essentially guarding the door to make sure no one interfered with Cindy and Derek's first actual connection. There would be no stupid "they're about to kiss and someone walks up to interrupt" things occurring. Those were always the most frustrating tropes in the movies.

But then I saw Axel heading toward the door at the same time as me.

Don't you dare! He was about to ruin everything!

Chapter 6

"Nope. No way, Mr. Rival," I insisted, turning toward Axel and placing both hands on his chest to prevent him from entering the hall. "You are not getting involved here, Axel." I pushed him past from the door and toward the wall instead, away from the crowd.

The young man stopped and tilted his head with a confused smirk, allowing me to move him with ease. "I'm going to see if Cindy's okay. I think I scared her."

"Yes, you did." I placed both hands on my hips, not wanting to touch him anymore now that we were out of the way. "You forced yourself on her and she's already skittish as it is. What were you thinking?"

Now Axel was frowning. "I wasn't forcing myself on her. I leaned in for a kiss, she said no, and I let her go. I was only following her to apologize. Do you really think I'd force a second kiss after she rejected the first? What kind of a jerk do you think I am?"

I scoffed. "I know your reputation, Axel Burns, and you're not going near my friend ever again. She has enough problems as it is." I shook my head and turned away. "Honestly, trying to kiss her before asking her out on a date. She's not that type of girl."

He stopped smirking for a moment, taking my words in, then sighed and looked up at the ceiling. "I don't know what you've heard about me, Zilla Yahui," he said, mimicking my use of the full name for emphasis. "But I have zero plans to hurt Cindy. I'm not some rapist or something. I asked her out because she was cute and sweet to me. I don't have ulterior motives here, and if she's not interested I'll leave her alone. I don't need to force girls to be with me. I have plenty of other options in case you haven't noticed." His jawline stuck out. He must be gritting his teeth in genuine frustration. No more fake smiles here. "I'd appreciate it if you didn't lash out at me for things I didn't do."

Now *I* was the one taking deep breaths to calm down. He was right. I hadn't seen what happened and was judging him solely based on rumors. Cindy had been right about me. I was being too judgmental. "Okay," I whispered, too stubborn in the moment to apologize. I should give him a break, but this party was giving me a headache and I was too excited about Cindy's development to focus on Axel.

"...Good." Axel looked past me at the hallway entrance. "May I go?"

"After Cindy?" I shook my head. He may not be a total creep, but I still didn't want him to ruin my plans. "No."

"Look, she might be crying. Either you go in there to talk to her or I will. I don't want her prom to become a sour memory."

I sighed. He had no idea what kind of genre we were in. "Derek's talking to her right now so I think she's fine."

"Derek Daniels?" He blinked rapidly, confusion showing on his face. "Sam's boyfriend?"

"Not for long." I grinned, then looked over my shoulder at the hallway. "Fine. I'll check on her. Just..." I made a shooing motion toward him. "Go find some other girl to dance with."

"Will you update me on what happened, at least?" he asked. "I still want to apologize."

"Okay." If he was being genuine, I couldn't fault him for it. "If I see you again, I'll let you know, okay?" I softened my voice just a bit. If his heart was in the right place, I'd give him a break.

He smiled again, directing it at me this time and doing it in a way that crinkled his eyes. I hated that he was using that seductive grin on me right after he used it on Cindy. "Now go, please," I added. *Before I reveal to you that we're all part of a book where Cindy is the main character and you're the villain.*

As he headed back into the crowd and immediately zeroed in on a different pretty girl to dance with, I turned away and headed down the hall. When I turned a corner, I found Cindy and Derek sitting together, chatting and laughing like they were supposed to.

Once I knew things were going well, I backed away unnoticed and headed back to the prom room. I still acted as a guard, but I didn't ruin the moment. If something went wrong, I would be within earshot and could intervene.

A small flash of loneliness struck me as I stood in the corner, arms crossed and alone. It was brief, and it was better than dancing with some guy I didn't know, but the feeling was there all the same.

At least Axel was out of the picture for now. That was the real takeaway here. Everything should go smoothly from now on.

That was how I comforted myself for the next hour. It would be smooth sailing from here. That was all that mattered.

Chapter 7

"So let me get this straight," I said to Cindy one week after prom. We were seated in a small fast-food joint near the high school. The scent of hot oil and melting ice cream filled the cool air.

The dance happened last week but since midterms occurred right after, we'd barely had time to chat in-depth about the Derek thing. Hence, I invited her to this restaurant as soon as we had free time so I could interrogate her fully. "You talked to him all night, bonded over your love of spaghetti—"

"Macaroni and cheese," Cindy corrected as we munched on French fries together.

"Macaroni and cheese," I amended. "And then he walked you to your dad's car..."

"Yup." She was beaming.

"And...." I waited for her to continue but she never did.

She paused, a fry hovering in front of her mouth. "And what?"

"And what happened after that?"

"What do you mean? Nothing else happened."

"Nothing? Then why haven't you spoken to him since? It's been a whole week." I had assumed something went wrong since nothing had developed after that night. Maybe Derek refused to leave Samantha or something, despite his obvious chemistry with Cindy. I don't know. That would be honorable of him, at least.

I'd played out scenarios in my head all week, so it felt wrong to hear Cindy say that nothing of the sort had happened. The sole reason I'd avoided bringing up the subject before was because I thought things went poorly between them. Why else would they be avoiding each other?

"I know." Cindy fiddled with the fry, squeezing it between her fingers. "We just...haven't had the chance to...I don't know. He hasn't made an effort to talk to me. That means he's not interested, right? Plus, he has a girlfriend."

"Samantha?" I shrugged. "She's not into him." Not anymore, at least, after how he acted at prom. "I have it on good authority that her and Timothy are getting together soon anyway." I blew my hair out of my face, glad we were on the same page now. It was time to jumpstart the next step now that Samantha was out of the picture. "Well, if he's not talking to you, *you* have to make the first move."

"I don't know." She was looking down now, so obnoxiously shy. I loved her, but this was so frustrating. "He's so good looking and funny and I'm so..."

"Kind and loveable. Cindy, he adores you. Why else would he comfort you during prom? It's just..."

My own words trailed off as I saw the restaurant door open and Derek himself walk in with Samantha, Axel, and Timothy in tow. What a coincidence. Also, what a strange group. Didn't the author think it was odd for those four to be hanging out? Sam and Derek made sense. They were supposed to be dating. Even Sam and Timothy made sense. But all four at the same time in one group? It felt so contrived.

Axel spotted me on his way to the counter and winked at me as he passed, chewing gum while he smiled in my direction. However, when Derek spotted Cindy sitting across from me with her back turned, he started getting all jumpy. He had that lovestruck, "unable to focus on anyone but her" look in his eyes. Perfect.

"It's just that you need to be more assertive," I finished, smiling to myself as the group sat down at the other end of the building. "He's probably shy like you and thinks you don't like him, just like you're thinking the same about him." With an unbridled smirk, I nodded past her shoulder. "Now's the perfect chance to talk to him. He just walked in." I'd always wanted to have one of these moments and now it was here!

Cindy's eyes looked ready to pop out when she glanced over her shoulder, spotted Derek, and immediately turned back to me with a face like a tomato. "We need to leave," she hissed.

"You literally just said you wanted to talk to him. Now's your chance." I was going to do anything short of shoving her across the room to get them together. Perhaps there was a way I could get Axel away from the group too. Then Timothy could flirt with Sam and Derek could take my seat here.

"He's with Samantha," Cindy added, her breaths quickening from panic.

"They're sitting as far away from each other as possible," I countered. "I don't think they're dating anymore." Again, why was he even with those three if he and Samantha didn't get along? It was so uncreative and illogical for the author to make them form a group. "Listen, if you don't go and talk to them, I will."

I waited for her to move but when she didn't—she was too busy biting her lip and staring out the window—I rolled my eyes the way a dramatic best friend would and got up with a loud scrape of the chair. I had to admit, I was playing into my role a little more than I should. I wasn't normally so assertive. It was only when it came to the storyline that I acted like this.

However, a girl has to do what a girl has to do (to advance the plot and avoid silly encounters).

"Miss Yahui," Axel greeted me with a grin as I approached them. He looked particularly bright and cheery today. Maybe it was because of the weekend break. That or I was just becoming more aware of him and his looks. "To what do we owe the pleasure?"

I still disliked him but at least his charisma made things less awkward. The others certainly weren't helping. Samantha glared at me as soon as we made eye contact and Derek avoided looking my way. Only Timothy gave a polite smile. He clearly hadn't forgotten my rejection last week.

"Actually, I was just sitting over there and noticed you four walk in," I said, nodding at my table and Cindy's slouched figure. "How are you?"

"Just swell," Axel said.

"Would you like to join us?" Timothy added politely. He'd stolen some of Axel's charm, it seemed. That or he was just trying to impress Samantha, who still looked pissed for reasons only slightly unknown. Derek was still in the bumbling male lead mode.

"Thanks for the invitation, but no. I actually came over because I need to talk to you about the school project we're working on together, Axel," I said pointedly.

"School project?" He glanced at his friends, then realization dawned on him and he nodded. "Right. Right. That." He immediately got to his feet and stood beside me. Strange. He felt much taller now than he did when we were in the cafeteria. "But your friend over there shouldn't be left alone, right?"

"Right." He was playing along well. It was almost like he knew the reality we were in. "Derek, why don't you go sit with my friend Cindy? You two have English together and she's having trouble with the essay that's due next week." I was lying, of course, but knew Derek would say yes regardless of which assignments were due.

"Uh...Okay." Derek looked both terrified and relieved. "Sure."

Timothy shot me a grateful look as I left him alone with Samantha. Meanwhile, Derek walked up to Cindy with a slow gait and Axel and I sat in a far corner where I could keep an eye on both couples. I didn't even bother bringing my food from the original table with me. Cindy and Derek didn't need any more interruptions.

"So," Axel began as I pulled out my wallet to buy myself another drink. "Tell me about this project we're working on."

"The project," I said, pulling out a five-dollar bill, "is sitting here and pretending to talk while I help my friend with her love life." As long as Axel wasn't a rival, I didn't care what he did. He could flirt with all the girls he wanted as long as it wasn't with me or Cindy.

"I see." Axel frowned in amused confusion as I got up yet again to purchase a cola. "Whatever you say."

Chapter 8

"So, Zilla," Axel began when I joined him again at the table. My paper straw was already melting into my soda and I was focusing on drinking as much of it as I could. He didn't seem to mind all my sipping as he leaned forward, his hands resting on top of the table between us. "That's an odd name. What's it stand for? Not Godzilla, I imagine."

I tried not to tense up at his joke. "If you must know," I began, peering over his shoulder at Cindy, who was laughing at something Derek said. "My real name is Xiang Yahui but I—uh—my dad gave me a nickname and it kind of stuck—." I could tell he wasn't quite buying it, which made sense since it wasn't the whole truth. I caved. "Well, *I* chose the nickname but—"

Axel smirked. "And you chose Zilla because...?"

I paused and gulped. I didn't want to answer that. I usually got away with just claiming my dad did it, but this guy could read me like a book.

Axel lowered his head. He wasn't flirting now. He was suppressing a laugh. "You *did* name yourself after Godzilla, didn't you?"

Dang it, why did he have to be right? Yes, I named myself after Godzilla! The monster looked like a dinosaur, and I loved dinosaurs at the time! "Well, what did they name *you* after? A tool?"

"The axle you're referring to is spelled differently," he explained, that amused light never leaving his eyes. "But I know you were just looking for an excuse to call me a tool so I'll pretend you were right."

My, he was good at leading the conversation. Too bad I wasn't interested...mostly.

Cindy laughed again at something Derek said and I couldn't help smiling in satisfaction. Cindy and Derek's relationship felt like a part of me, like I was the fairy godmother. I suppose I technically was.

Axel smiled when I did. "So, once those two start dating, what are you planning to do?"

"Relax and focus on my studying," I answered easily, since I'd already thought it through.

"And you won't be angry about losing your best friend to a guy?" he asked.

"No, of course not. We won't stop being friends just because she has a boyfriend." At least I hoped so. "Besides, she's been obsessed with him for months now, so this won't change much."

He shrugged. "I thought the same until my best friend got a girlfriend. Now I talk to him once every two months. He's always out with his girl on some date and when he's not *with* her, he's texting her."

"Are you referring to Timothy?" Was Timothy planning to cheat on his girlfriend with Sam?

"No, not him. Timothy's chasing Samantha anyway, which I think you've already noticed." Oh, good. "No, my best bud goes to school in Brighton."

Ah. "That explains your accent." His English accent was so subtle I barely noticed it until just now. If it was any stronger, he would have fit yet another stereotype—the hot, blonde, British playboy. Those stories usually ended up with him secretly being royalty or something, though.

"Hardly." He shrugged. "I moved here when I was eight and only one of my parents grew up there."

Wait. I let my mouth slam shut as I realized we were we having an actual conversation and I was letting him lead it with that flirty tone of his. A week ago, he was flirting with my best friend. Now he was doing it to me. I shouldn't allow that, even if he was a little fun to talk to.

I redirected my attention toward the brown cola and focused on how there was too much ice in it and not enough liquid. Hopefully the silence would send a message that I'd had enough of talking.

Unfortunately, Axel knew he had me trapped at this table and wasn't deterred by obvious silences. "So, tell me about your life dreams, Godzilla. Matchmaking can't be your only aspiration, can it? I'm sure there's money in it but—"

"I want to be a nurse," I grumbled, pissed off by the nickname he'd used *and* his assertions.

"A nurse?" He smirked again. "...Interesting."

"It's not interesting at all, is it?" I asked, not really annoyed by his tone this time since *I* didn't think highly of the profession either. Plenty of girls went into nursing. It was perfectly normal, albeit not the most interesting.

"It's respectable." He looked ready to reach for my drink so I pulled it away. "It suits you."

"Oh, does it?" I couldn't resist the eye roll. If it suited me, did that mean he considered *me* boring? "What's your future plan then? Inheriting a business from your parents? Lawyer? Real estate?"

"I can see you've put me solidly into the rich boy box," he answered, matching my sarcasm perfectly. "And to answer your question, none of the above. I want to be a teacher."

That was surprising. I shifted in my chair. "Teaching what?"

"English. I plan to go abroad. Don't know where yet."

"...Interesting."

"Now you're saying it back to me." He paused, taking a moment to practice mimicking my voice accurately. "It's not interesting at all, is it?" he asked, repeating my line.

He was frustrating to talk to, though then again, so was I. I tended to be sarcastic and could tell he was mirroring me. "It's just...hard to picture, that's all," I said quietly.

"Well, it's just a temporary goal. I plan to do it for a few years, see a bit of the world, then go to school again to study something else. I figure I'll know myself better by then."

"How respectable." And I meant it. "So I take it you're not rich then?" That didn't fit the stereotype. The only other stereotype to match would be if *Derek* was secretly rich, which I didn't think he was. His dad was one of the teachers at our school and his mom edited for our small-town magazine.

"You're really determined to figure out if I'm rich or not." He leaned forward again, uncomfortably close this time. "Why are you so curious, Xiang Yahui?"

I was impressed he'd pronounced the name so well right off the bat. The fact that he remembered me at all had improved my opinion of him.

Also, he was too close, and his tricks weren't working on me. "I just assumed a guy like you would also be rich. It would explain your whole..." I gestured toward his entire body. "You."

I said it with a playful tone, but he leaned away, his smile dropping, and his hands started fiddling with the salt and pepper shakers on the table. Now *he* was giving me the awkward silence. I must have genuinely hurt his feelings.

Dang it. Now I felt bad.

I saw movement out of the corner of my eye and sat up, eager for a way out.

Oh! Cindy was getting up. Perfect! Time to go! Thank goodness. I could avoid this awkwardness and hopefully never speak to Axel again. "Thanks for the help, Axel," I said and rushed to flee the situation. Befriending Axel wasn't a goal of mine anyway, even if I was a little attracted to him.

Guilt still clung to me on the way back to Cindy's table. I wished I hadn't put my foot in my mouth like that. Axel was being nice to me, and I'd hurt his feelings. Sure, it fit my sarcastic best friend stereotype perfectly, but that didn't mean I had to like it.

But it was too late to apologize now and Cindy looked desperate to leave so I went after her. I was sure Axel would get over it quickly. He seemed like the type to bounce back fast.

Chapter 9

To my great relief, my little matchmaking scheme in the restaurant worked.

In the coming weeks, Derek became comfortable enough to join Cindy and me at our lunch table.

When it became obvious that Derek's visits were going to be a regular thing, I turned into the ultimate third wheel. Their quick friendship immediately led into flirtation, which made things uncomfortable very quickly. I eventually resorted to bringing my textbooks to the lunch table so I'd have an excuse to back out of the conversation without completely abandoning Cindy.

Axel never joined us, which was to be expected, but a tiny part of me wished things were how they'd been in the restaurant, with Cindy and Derek talking alone while Axel and I did the same. Anything was preferable to feeling left out of my own friend group. However, I'd be a fool to invite Axel to join us after what I said to him. I wasn't sure why the thought of inviting him even entered my mind.

Unfortunately, I still felt bad about what I said to Axel, and it took weeks to get over the guilt. I convinced myself I hadn't done anything wrong when I insulted him and he was just sulking, but even after telling myself things were fine, the memory of his disappointed face never left my mind.

Luckily, my guilt didn't have much time to linger. The third quarter exams began and they distracted me right away. Good grades were my priority, even if they weren't mandatory to get accepted into university.

Plus, Axel started very publicly dating that blonde from prom, the one wearing silver who replaced Cindy, so it was clear a simple insult from me wasn't consuming his thoughts. Why should he care what a girl like me thought of him when he had such a beautiful one on his arm?

That meant my worries could swing back to Cindy and Derek's relationship again—after I passed my exams with moderately good grades, of course. The pair had been hanging out as friends for almost a month now and I could tell Cindy was getting anxious because Derek hadn't asked her out yet. He was friend-zoning her, and it clearly had her worried that he wasn't fully interested. Sure, all the signs of a crush were there, but Cindy's insecurities always managed to block them out.

I gave it one more week, then finally did something about it. I wasn't planning to tell Cindy to make the first move this time, since Derek was close enough now that he had no excuse. He had to stop being a coward! If *I* had been willing to make conversation with both Axel and Samantha at the drop of a hat, *he* could ask out the girl he'd liked for nearly a year.

That was how I ended up cornering Derek in the library a few days later. I had spotted him through the door when passing by and decided on the spur of the moment to enter, pretending I was there to study. Now that exams were over, I had more time to interfere with their love life again.

"Zilla," Derek greeted me with that dimpled smile as I approached him. He was sitting at one of the far corner tables, a few biology books strewn about and his phone resting face-down atop one of them. "I was just studying. Do you want to join me?"

I clearly did, but not to study.

He kept smiling as I sat down across from him, but the grin faded as I immediately began interrogating him without a proper segue. "I'm here to figure out why you haven't asked Cindy out on a date yet."

His smile faltered and he slumped down in his chair. "I'm sorry but...that's not really any of your business."

"So, you don't plan to ask her out?" I asked doubtfully, making myself comfortable across the table but keeping my books in my bag for now. "I thought you liked her."

"I do but..." He sighed and leaned away. "I want to take my time. I don't want to rush into this and ruin everything by being too eager."

Understandable, but Cindy wouldn't feel the same way. "I think a month is more than enough time to get to know each other as friends," I interjected, aware of how pushy I sounded, but the *plot* was at stake. If this kept up, Cindy might fall into the arms of another seductive playboy. I wouldn't put it past the author to use that trope twice in a row. "It's clear you two like each other. You should snatch her up before someone else decides to beat you to the punch."

His eyes widened, then narrowed, and he sat up in his seat. The scowl on his face made me realize I'd said the wrong thing yet again. This whole book business was beginning to interfere with my common sense.

"Can I be honest with you, Zilla?"

"...Sure." Now I was the one leaning away. I gulped, getting déjà vu from my conversation with Axel.

"You're a little too overprotective and nosy when it comes to Cindy."

My heart lurched, in part because he was right, and I hated to hear it confirmed.

"I do plan to ask her out but I'd really prefer you not get involved. The main reason I haven't done it yet is because ninety-nine percent of the time, *you're* always with us."

Another good point.

This was humiliating.

"So if you'd just leave us to it and—I don't know—not get involved, I'd really appreciate it." He was saying it sweetly, like a dog who'd been kicked, and I felt guilty once again.

"I'm sorry, Derek."

He shrugged and shook his head. I must look so annoying in his eyes. Heck, now that I'd settled down a little bit, I was annoyed at myself.

"It's okay," he said. "I'm just glad we discussed it now before it became a serious problem."

"I'll try to stay out of your way," I said meekly as he packed up his books to avoid the stifling atmosphere.

"Sounds good." He gave me a halfway smile, then headed out.

Maybe he was right. I *was* being a pushy, annoying, and almost smothering figure in Cindy's life. I really should learn my place. It turned out the real drama preventing their relationship was *me*. How ironic.

"And you thought *I* was the rude one."

I jumped in my seat. That familiar voice behind me belonged to Axel. What was he doing here? Had the author put him there? If so, why?

I turned around slowly as he appeared from behind one of the bookshelves. He had a dictionary in hand, but it was upside down. I understood why a moment later, as a girl walked past who must have been with him. She wasn't blonde and definitely wasn't his girlfriend. How scandalous. The girl he'd been cheating with snuck away as Axel took a seat next to me and gestured toward Derek's back.

"I take it your matchmaking isn't going as planned?"

"I'm not a matchmaker," I answered, frowning. "And no. It's not," I admitted quietly.

"Do you want my help?" He leaned back in his chair, looking quite handsome and drawing attention from a few other girls seated nearby. "Or do you think you have this handled? What with your...marvelous way with words."

"I don't need to hear your insults right now, Axel. I've heard enough of them from Derek for one day." I sighed and rested my head on my fist, trying to will my heart to stop pounding so fast.

"Well, luckily for you, I'm not as easy to annoy as he apparently is."

"Really?" I hesitated, knowing I was about to put my foot in my mouth again, then decided I should test what he'd just bragged about. "You seemed pretty annoyed last time we spoke."

"No. My feelings were hurt. Derek, on the other hand, was pissed. Those are completely different emotions."

Great. Now I felt bad again for hurting him. I tried to frown but failed and tried to change the subject instead. "Anyway, Derek wasn't annoyed. He was right. I'm like a mother hen when it comes to Cindy. I should stop third wheeling so much."

"But he *was* a little rude, you have to admit. Look," Axel paused and leaned forward like he did last time—before I practically called him a prick. "Here's what I can do. I can flirt with Cindy a little bit and make Mr. Derek slightly jealous. Then he'll feel threatened, finally ask her out, and you can stop stressing about their love life."

Now *I* was pissed. "And how will your girlfriend feel if she sees you flirting with Cindy?" I asked. "She might take it out on Cindy instead of you. Plus, I don't want my best friend's heart being messed with." She was already confused about Derek. We didn't need to add more factors into the mix.

"My girlfriend won't care since our relationship isn't serious and even if she does get mad, we can just break up," he said, waving his hand in the air like his relationship didn't matter. "And my flirting won't be genuine. I would never pursue a girl after she rejected me. It's rude and borderline creepy."

"I agree, which is why you flirting with her again isn't a good idea."

"Note the word *genuine*. I'll just flatter her a little, make a show of being nice to her, then let the rumors do the rest. What's the harm in it? It'll just be an act to get Derek jealous, right? Once my job is done, I'll back off again."

I bit my lip. "It would be very fitting for the plot," I muttered to myself. He was the rival, after all. Making the male lead jealous was his job. Plus, I would rather Axel pretend to flirt than have a new playboy character insert himself and get attached to Cindy.

But it was still a bad idea for a plethora of reasons.

"The plot? Are you writing a book about this or something?" His mouth quirked. "That would explain why you're so invested in their—"

"No!" *Dang it. I said the part about the book out loud, didn't I?* "Fine. Do it, but if anything goes wrong, I'm blaming you."

He bowed dramatically. "I shall take all the blame." Then he flashed a bright grin my way and my blasted, stupid heart skipped a beat. Luckily, I immediately recalled the girl who walked out from behind the bookshelf a moment ago and my heart beat properly again. "However, there is the subject of payment. What am I getting in return for my sacrifice?"

"Sacrifice?" I laughed. "You flirt with girls all the time. This won't inconvenience you in the slightest."

"Like I said, flirting with a girl who already rejected me is against my code." He drew out the last word, waiting for my answer. "Plus, Derek and I are friends. It would be pretty scummy of me to flirt with his girl."

I sighed and leaned back in the chair, mimicking his earlier stance. "She's not his girl yet, hence the jealousy act. What do you want from me? Money? Food? A movie ticket?"

"I was thinking more along the lines of...a date."

Oh no. I saw where this was going. I'd heard that cliché line plenty of times in rom-coms.

I recoiled.

Since I was a side character and side romances were popular in books, I bet the author planned for me to fall for this playboy so it could lead into a heartbreak storyline where he would cheat and Cindy would have to console me.

No thank you.

"Money or nothing," I said. "And I won't go over ten dollars. I don't have a job."

He caught my drift quickly and shrugged. "How about we do an 'I owe you' instead."

"Deal, but my rules won't change."

"Sure." He winked at me, then sauntered off on his new mission to help Cindy. I, meanwhile, had to remind myself that he had a girlfriend, even though that wink made me feel things I didn't want to experience.

Chapter 10

By Monday, Derek had asked Cindy out to the movies. He did it after he allegedly saw Axel flirt with her next to the lockers. Everyone was talking about it, since the students at our high school loved gossip. This was a small town, after all. They took what entertainment they could get.

The next day, I found an IOU note in my locker, signed by Axel with a quaint little heart beside his signature. It felt like he was mocking me.

When I passed Axel in the hall an hour later, I didn't mention the note. I did, however, notice a pink mark on his face from a presumed slap his girlfriend gave him. She was probably the first to hear about his flirtation. I was surprised she *hadn't* learned about all the other girls he "hung out with" in the library before that. Or maybe this was just the last humiliating straw that broke the camel's back. Either way, she probably dodged a bullet. Dating a cheater would only bring her more heartache down the line. Best to pull off that band-aid now.

I hoped Axel wouldn't actually cash in on that IOU because I didn't feel like giving him any money. I thought he deserved the slap, regardless of our agreement. He'd had it coming for a while now.

Once Cindy and Derek became an official couple, I saw Cindy less and less. Her weekends were spent with Derek instead of me and half of our lunch hours were spent apart too. I found the table where Cindy and I had always eaten together empty half the time. It reached a point where after I grabbed my food, I walked straight to the library instead and claimed a nice green chair in the corner behind some shelves where the librarians couldn't see me eat.

As the weeks passed and the solitude became routine, I began to admit one thing. Even though I preferred isolation to being an unwanted third wheel, Axel had been right about the loneliness. The library lunch hours offered a good opportunity to study…but they also reminded me of just how alone I truly was. Did I really have no other friends in this school besides Cindy? The closest were some study buddies in my math class and they had their own cliques to join during lunch. I could always force my way into their groups, but it would be at least a little awkward to insert myself without an invitation.

Luckily the lunch hours, while still lonely, weren't boring. There was always something to keep me distracted, or rather someone, and that someone's name started with the letters A and B. The library was Axel Burns' favorite place to bring ladies, as I quickly learned, and unfortunately I had to see seven different girls flirt with him over the following month. His little escapades behind the bookshelves were sadly right in my line of sight from the green chair. I didn't see any making out actually occur, thank goodness, but had to watch him enter and exit his secret location every week. I considered moving from my spot several times, but the chair was so comfortable and private that it made me stubborn. Why should I be the one to move just because he wanted to mess around with girls? He should be the one to leave, not me!

I told him so after the seventh girl left. Instead of exiting the library a minute after his lady did, Axel started touring the comic book aisle at the back of the library. Seeing him do so, I decided to have a chat with him about his location choice. There were still a few months left before graduation and I didn't want to see him reach double digits by the time that event rolled around.

So, as he pulled a Wolfman comic from the shelf to study the helmeted character on the cover, I stepped in front of him. My bookbag was clutched in front of me for protection just in case he tried to lean in too close, as he often did when attempting to make me uncomfortable.

"Hello, Axel," I said, my voice calm and firm.

He looked up from his book and immediately grinned at me. "Godzilla! It's been a while. How have you been? I haven't seen you in forever."

"Yes, of course you haven't," I muttered. He'd only walked past me seven different times this month. But that wasn't the point. I shouldn't care if he noticed me or not, especially when he had a pretty, giggling girl on his arm. "I have a request to make."

"Oh?" He leaned against the bookshelf coolly and motioned for me to continue, swinging the book at me. "Do tell. You still owe me for last time. If this is yet another request, you'll owe me double."

"Right." Dang it, I'd nearly forgotten about that and wished he hadn't reminded me. I frowned and pulled a strand of hair behind my ear, delaying so I could think things through. "Well, that can't be avoided. Besides, this second request won't inconvenience you." Not like that slap from his ex-girlfriend did. "It's about your choice of make out spots, mainly this one." I pointed at the corner where he always hid with his girls.

"It's the only one I need," he said, like he was bragging. "Perfect spot. No one can see or hear us, but we won't look suspicious if we get caught." He held both hands over the spot like he was taking a picture of it, then tilted his head back toward me. "Why? You don't approve?"

"Of course I don't approve!"

"Of the making out itself or the location?" He feigned innocence and batted his eyelashes at me.

I clenched my jaw. "I don't care what you do, Axel, but I'd appreciate it if you didn't do it *here*. I always sit in that chair during lunch and have to keep seeing you..." I cringed and chose not to finish that sentence. "Can you do it somewhere else, please?"

"Well, what would you recommend?" He leaned a little closer, just as I feared he would. "Where do you normally take the boys *you're* interested in?"

"That's disgusting. Don't assume everyone acts like you."

He didn't look offended by my comment. If anything, he looked amused. "I don't know of any other spots—"

"An alley, behind the convenience store next door, behind the school. Just anywhere other than where I'm trying to study, okay?" I raised my hands in exasperation and turned to leave. "It's distracting."

"Oh? I'm distracting?" I could hear the smile on his lips even though I wasn't facing him anymore. "Does it bother you to see me with other girls?"

Red flag. That was something a book character would say. "Making out shouldn't happen inside the school, okay? It's *gross*." I put emphasis on the last word to ensure he knew it was a matter of vomiting rather than blushing. "Please, just do it somewhere else. I want to spend my final months here in peace."

"Okay," he said as I left, soft and quiet. There was no more sarcasm, though it was likely because I was already on my way out.

When he gave in without making a big deal of it, I paused at the edge of the bookshelves and looked back. "Thanks, Axel. I appreciate it."

His eyes lit up slightly, but I avoided looking at them any longer. I wanted to get out of here before he cashed in that IOU.

I could already feel a load fall off my chest now that I'd been straight with him. Hopefully he'd do as I asked and promptly forget about his earlier favor while he was at it.

Chapter 11

I never saw Axel again during our final months of high school and thanks to that, my grades rose considerably. I ended up having a perfect 4.0 GPA by the time exams rolled around. I also kept an eye on Cindy's grades too, though I tried not to be overbearing since I didn't want to interfere like Derek said I had.

Everything was going smoothly until, two weeks before graduation, my mundane schedule changed yet again.

"Do you mind?" Axel asked as he pulled a plastic blue chair up to my fabric green one in the library. I'd been in the midst of reading a bland Shakespeare book and pretending to enjoy it when he showed up. "Of course you don't," he added and slammed the chair down beside me before I could even get a word out. "How have you been, Godzilla?"

"I have a 4.0 GPA and Cindy's in a wonderful relationship thanks to you," I answered, only smiling slightly as he crossed his legs and reclined in the seat like he owned the place. What did he want? "And I don't need to ask how you've been doing because I see it every day, or rather *who* you've been doing." He had stayed out of sight, just as promised, but I still passed him in the halls sometimes and knew he was keeping himself busy. He probably felt the need to rush through these last couple of "relationships" because high school was coming to an end.

"Yes, yes." He waved my words away. "Not my fault you decided to station yourself in my territory during our final year. So." He peered at the book I'd been reading, then looked back up at me. "You owe me double now…"

"I know." I sighed and waited. "What is it you want, then?"

"I'm so glad you asked, Zilla. Now, what do I want? Hmm. I want…" He paused, drawing this out. "I want to know what university you're going to," he finally said and snickered when he saw my shocked expression. "I'm curious."

"That's all you want in return for that slap?" I almost felt bad for him now.

"Oh, the slap was unrelated to you and Cindy." Word of his cheating must have gotten to her before his flirting with Cindy did, just as I suspected. "So, what school will you be attending?"

He didn't seem to have an ulterior motive, so I lowered my guard. "You can't make fun of me for it, okay?"

"Deal."

"I'm going to a school in Ontario," I said slowly.

"Canada? Why?"

"Because that's where Cindy is going to get her teaching degree. She says the teaching jobs there are pretty good and pay more than American ones, plus she has dual citizenship."

He tilted his head. "You chose your university based on where Cindy was going?"

"With my grades, I can go anywhere I want, and nursing isn't exactly a niche thing," I countered. It admittedly sounded weird now that he said it like that.

"They'll charge you more if you're not a citizen." But he was smirking now, intrigued. "And what about Derek? Is he going there too?"

"Yes. He has family up there, so it was an easy choice for him." It was all very contrived, but I expected no less from our terrible author.

Axel took a moment to absorb this information, then released a deep breath.

"What?" I asked, preparing to be insulted.

"I don't know. I just think it might be...good for you to go where *you* want to go."

"I *want* to go to Ottawa. Is that so hard to believe? You don't know me very well. How would you know what I want?" He was beginning to sound like Derek. "Besides, Cindy needs me to watch over her."

"...Really?"

I mean, maybe she didn't but...

Well, he just didn't get it. He didn't understand that it was my *job* to be by her side. It was my role in life. The college arc needed the best friend there to help the main character navigate through adult hardships. Besides...Cindy was my only friend. These last few months had proved it. What if I moved to a university and couldn't make any new friends? I didn't like the thought of being alone all over again. It felt...frankly, awful.

"Well, I wish you luck on your journey," Axel said finally. "And you still owe me that date. If you want to cash it in now—"

"You'd be the one cashing it in," I reminded him, "and thank you but no. I don't want to become girl number eight from the library."

"Number eight? You've been keeping count?"

"Thank you, Axel. I'm leaving." I'd had enough.

He chuckled as I exited, having fun at my expense. Thank goodness I'd be a country away from him a few months from now.

Chapter 12

I must admit, I was quite relieved when graduation rolled around. While the high school chapter of my life wasn't particularly awful, it wasn't really noteworthy either. Most of it was spent with books rather than people, and I hadn't formed any long-term memories to recall fondly. I hoped university would prove to be different but didn't have my hopes up.

At least the ceremony went well. It took place inside our gymnasium, with the basketball hoops lifted and bleachers replaced with rows upon rows of metal chairs. While the event wasn't anything special, I got to sit next to Cindy during all the speeches and we had plenty of fun trying to predict the principal's words. Some of the things we guessed he'd say were beyond ridiculous. Making jokes with Cindy reminded me how much I missed spending time with her one-on-one.

Once the diplomas were handed out and our square caps were off, we were escorted out of the gym so parents could congratulate their students and take pictures of them outside. Cindy and I were separated quickly. I had to watch from the sidelines as she met up with her parents, then rejoined Derek so she could meet his mother too.

I, meanwhile, was left alone next to an outdoor table covered with donuts and fruit trays. My parents had intended to be there, but plans changed when my little brother got sick that morning and needed to be taken to the hospital to make sure it wasn't anything serious. He'd always had a weak heart as a baby, so his health came first over my own personal accomplishments. I didn't mind it. His safety was our family's priority.

I eventually settled down in a plastic chair in the shade of a tree, enjoying the general splendor and excitement in the air, but the peace was broken when I heard the dragging of another chair being pulled over to me. I was struck with a strong sense of déjà vu.

Sure enough, it was just who I expected: Axel. He'd already taken off his black cap and gown to show off a tight red shirt and jeans underneath. His hair was swept back, nicely trimmed for the occasion. He looked put together for once.

"I was hoping to meet your parents," he joked as he cocked his head toward me. "Mine couldn't make it."

I was struck with how similar we were to each other in this moment and forgot to answer for a few seconds. "Mine couldn't either," I finally said as he made himself comfortable. "My brother got sick."

"Mine just didn't show up. Graduation isn't a big deal unless it brings a degree." He sighed as he said it and I could tell it genuinely hurt him. "A lawyer and real estate agent make a pretty horrid combo when it comes to parenting. But at least you have Cindy, right?"

I was tempted to make some sassy comment, since I'd heard criticism of my overattachment to Cindy plenty of times already from Derek. But I knew Axel meant no harm. Plus, this was the last time I would ever see this guy, so there was no need to be mean.

"How do you think your university life will go?" he asked, voicing the question I'd been asking myself.

"I don't know. Hopefully better than my high school one," I answered honestly. "I'm hoping to make more friends after the move, though my personality doesn't exactly attract people."

"And why do you think that is?" Axel leaned toward me playfully, studying my face to see if I'd admit the truth.

I studied the crowd around us—all the students I had spent hours with inside classrooms. I'd spoken to each of them at least once, but anytime people tried to talk to me, I would either say very little or something very wrong. Sometimes my cliché sarcasm came back to bite me.

"I'm not very friendly," I admitted, not sure how to put my more complex feelings into words. I could be a hard person to be around and knew it. Cindy was more tolerant of me than others were.

"That's part of it, sure," Axel said. "You certainly haven't been friendly to me. Luckily, I have a thick skin."

I was both relieved and resentful that he'd just agreed with my observation. "You never seem to have trouble making friends," I admitted sadly. "What do you suggest I do to improve?" I was treating this like a school lesson, rather than a casual conversation.

"Well..." He looked like he was holding back a cheeky grin from having the upper hand. Then he matched my serious expression. "For now, just put in effort to make conversation and don't worry about what people think. Out of ten people, it's nearly impossible for every single one to dislike you, so don't be afraid to take the risk by starting a conversation. Oh, and be nice too. That's normally a given but I just wanted to make it clear."

Now that I thought about it, he was right. Nearly every conversation we'd had was started by him.

Axel paused so I could absorb his advice, then he added one more thing. "I think the best way to keep friends is to not pass judgement too easily. No one likes being put in a box or criticized right off the bat...including me."

He was clearly referring to how I had stuck him in a rich, playboy, jerk category when only one of those things ended up being right.

His words cut deep. I'd cast judgement on not only him and the people around me but on myself too. The "being in a book" thing was just an excuse to continue stereotyping everyone so I wouldn't have to think too hard about people or try to understand them.

"Right," I muttered, agreeing completely despite not wanting to admit I was prone to doing it.

"I'm surprised you asked me for advice," he said, looking content with the conversation's end. "I guess this new chapter will give us both a chance to rethink our lives."

As I sat there, doing just that, he leaned toward the buffet table and snagged a chocolate strawberry, looking quite pleased with himself. Meanwhile, I was seriously rethinking my life choices.

When his chomping of fruit began to annoy me, I spoke up again. "Axel?"

"Yup?" He turned toward me, cheeks bulging like a chipmunk. His playboy looks were gone now.

Seeing him look like that, so unlike the perfectly put-together appearance from before, released all my built-up tension and made me start laughing. My shoulders slouched as Axel stared at me like I was a crazy person.

"Sorry," I whispered, trying to wipe my eyes without messing up my mascara. "I think the stress is getting to me," I explained as I willed myself to stop giggling. It wasn't even that funny. It just felt nice to be on equal ground with him for once.

Sitting there next to him and realizing he was the only person to comfort me when I was alone, I almost wished this wouldn't be our last meeting. That was impossible, of course. We'd be in separate countries now, even if he'd only be a few states away. I could still picture it, though, just for a moment. What kind of a friendship would we have formed if we didn't separate? He could have ended up bringing out the best in me, like he was doing now.

I sighed. I wasn't even supposed to like the guy. Even if he was a nice person, he was still a cheater and flirt. Why was I wishing we could stay together a little longer?

I pushed away those silly wishes. At least we ended our relationship on a high note. Maybe someday we would meet again at a high school reunion, and I'd be a stronger, better person—someone who didn't rely on Cindy.

"Here." Axel handed me another strawberry and held up his own like we could toast them. "To making friends, right? Cheers?"

I sighed and gave in, allowing myself to act silly for just one moment. "To making friends."

He winked at me as we cheered our strawberries, ending our high school arc and going our separate ways.

PART TWO

Chapter 13

The trip to our new university in Canada was the most fun I had all year. Cindy and I made a little road trip of it without Derek or anyone else to interfere. Most of the ride was spent recounting funny stories, listening to humorous videos and CDs, and just singing along to silly kid songs we grew up with. It was a blast and a welcome escape from the nerves of entering a new city.

However, once we arrived and had to adjust to new people, classes, and the filling out of countless foreign documents, life became so busy that we barely had time to relax. Studying became an excuse to hang out together, which we often did in the university's massive library with its eight different floors. Even though most of our classes weren't shared anymore, we would still sit next to each other and study our textbooks or notes, sometimes without speaking for hours.

Everything was going smoothly...until someone arrived to switch things up.

On our first Saturday in the university, we were seated together in the library, reviewing our schedules and discussing which homework assignments we should prioritize during the semester. Well, *I* was doing most of the planning while Cindy was zoning out and people watching. I was knee deep in syllabuses when her voice cut through my focused thoughts.

"Is that Axel Burns?" Cindy asked. We were seated on the third floor of the library, resting on long leather seats. Twenty feet away from us was the path that led from the elevators to the study rooms and bookshelves. Lots of people passed by but none of them were familiar so I never paid attention to any of them. I didn't, that is, until Axel Burns himself walked past with a group of friends. I looked up and was shocked to see him stop in front of the elevator with some other students. He was laughing with his head angled up at the ceiling and mouth wide open, clearly enjoying himself.

What was he doing here?

How Cindy managed to spot Axel among all the other students in this crowded, loud space was beyond me. Why he was here at all was even more impossible to fathom, and I was so astonished that I decided to find out right then. People didn't just coincidentally end up in a university several states away from where they grew up, especially in another country.

The author's handiwork was written all over this.

"I'll be right back," I told Cindy, leaving my stuff on the bench and ignoring her confused but amused expression as I marched up to Axel and his crew.

He was in the midst of a group of four boys and six girls, several of whom made a point of focusing on him whenever they laughed. It appeared very little had changed. Good looks and charisma drew people to Axel regardless of age and location.

"Axel," I said, forcing a smile as I addressed him. "I never expected to see you here." Emphasis on the word *never*.

"Oh." His face lit up in a mischievous manner as he heard my voice and immediately identified me. "Sorry, guys, but I'll have to cut this conversation short. This is an old friend from high school. How have you been?" He immediately stepped closer to me, ignoring the confused stares the other girls directed my way. His tone made it sound like we were childhood friends who hadn't seen each other in years.

"Yes, it's been *so* long," I told Axel with a fake laugh. "A whole three months."

Axel smirked.

"But I'm glad you're here," I continued. "I need to talk to you about something, Axel." I didn't need to add the words "in private" for him to get the picture. I was sure he already knew what I planned to ask him. He didn't protest as I wrapped my hands around his arm and tugged him away.

"Of course." Axel continued grinning as he followed me to a different section of the library. I could feel Cindy's eyes on me as I went.

"So, you're going to school here too?" I asked, my smile disappearing as we stopped next to a window overlooking a series of sidewalks outside. There were still people around us, but none were close enough to hear our conversation. I would have preferred a private room to chat but there were few places in this massive university that were devoid of people, so I had to take what I could get.

I wanted to figure out what the author planned to do with Axel. Understanding *why* he came here in the first place would hopefully lead to that.

"Of course I am!" Axel answered enthusiastically. "I love traveling to foreign countries, and getting an English major here is super easy."

"Really?" I chuckled, releasing his arm and crossing my own. "And that's your only reason? I'd hardly call Canada foreign, by the way." Other than currency and a tiny bit of the culture, things felt pretty much the same.

"Of course," he repeated. "Why else would I come? Did you think I came here for you or something?"

No. What I *really* thought was that the author was too lazy to create a new rival for Derek, so she brought Axel along for some contrived reason. "No. I just think it's strange that you ended up here after using your favor to ask me where I was going to school."

"Coincidences are crazy, aren't they?" He laughed and I began to think he vehemently believed what he said. That meant the author truly couldn't come up with a real reason for him to show up. How lazy!

I decided at that moment that our author was the most unprofessional, amateur writer in North America. The longer I lived, the more astonished I became at his or her incompetence. This author's poor craft was already fairly obvious, with the pathetic attempts to force characters together despite it not making any sense. However, it became clear after arriving in Ottawa that the author was determined to keep her favorite group of four together—that group consisting of myself, Cindy, Derek, and the playboy rival Axel. Perhaps the author got attached to Axel's personality and couldn't let him go. That was common in the books I read, especially with characters who were meant to die off. The author would fall in love with them and keep them around despite it interfering with the planned plot.

I was about to continue my interrogation of Axel, wanting to make the author work for this crazy coincidence, when a new figure slipped into view.

"Axel." Derek appeared behind us. "What are you doing here?" He must have spotted his rival on the way in. That or Cindy told him as soon as he arrived.

...Or the author brought him in so I couldn't torment Axel with questions.

"I go to school here." The playboy turned his smile on the newcomer. Derek didn't look any more convinced than I was. "How's it going, Derek? How are you and Cindy doing?"

"That's...not really any of your business," Derek said quietly, looking a little protective of his girl. Good. Readers loved that stuff. No wonder the writer brought Axel along.

"I agree," I said, pulling Axel away from Derek. The air between them felt unpleasant, though it was mainly coming from Derek. I didn't blame the guy. Axel had flirted with his girl twice. Granted, both times Cindy had been single, but only an idiot would fail to realize she was unofficially taken. "Axel and I were just talking about the English class we share." I wanted to keep these two apart as much as possible.

"I see." Derek was still focused on Axel and didn't look too happy about his presence. It felt a little strange. They used to be friends, once upon a time. "You started going to school here, Axel?"

"Yeah." Axel grinned, sticking next to me and feigning ignorance.

"Small world, huh?" Derek was frowning now. Did he think Axel came all the way here to see Cindy or something? I mean, it was understandable. Axel *did* hit on her twice. Maybe Derek thought he was a stalker.

"It is indeed," Axel continued. "In fact—"

"He moved here to...be with me," I interrupted, knowing where this plot would go if Derek misunderstood any more. Miscommunication arcs were the most tedious things ever. It would cause a ton of jealousy and would definitely stress out Cindy. I couldn't allow that, even if I had to throw myself under the bus to avoid it.

Axel turned on me with wide eyes and an arm ready to wrap around my shoulders. "Yes, of course," he said. "We started dating during the summer and I just couldn't handle living five states away." He lied smoothly, immediately recognizing where this was going. At least he wasn't dumb. I'd owe him again, though, which would suck. I hated being indebted to people, especially when the payment was apparently a cliché date.

So, we were fake dating now. Great. I sighed quietly, then glanced at Derek to see if he was buying it. This was so typical. I had fallen right into this dumb author's hands.

"Right," I said, raising my chin and gritting my teeth in a forced smile. "We got close over the summer."

"I never heard anything about that. Why didn't you tell Cindy?" Derek asked.

Shoot! I told Cindy everything! Well, everything except for my growing dislike of Derek's attitude. "I didn't want to tell her since...you know, what happened at prom..." I cringed, hating the weight of Axel's hand on my left shoulder. "Could you keep it quiet from Cindy for now? This probably won't last long anyway." I pointed at Axel. "You know how he is. He can't stay loyal to anyone for longer than a month, so I don't think Cindy needs to know about it. This is just a fling."

Axel looked a little hurt that I had referenced his short relationships, but Derek believed it immediately. I wasn't sure if I should be offended that he didn't question why I was dating someone like Axel. Did he think I was easy or something? Or even worse—desperate?

"Okay. Just...don't be so public, then." Derek shook his head and prepared to walk in Cindy's direction. Then he paused and squinted at me. "Why are you dating him if you know it won't last long? You never struck me as the type to do that."

Shoot! He'd asked about it after all. Why couldn't he be as clueless as Cindy?

I was partly relieved that he'd asked, since it meant I didn't look as frivolous as I'd originally feared, but I also didn't have a proper answer. "Oh, I'm just trying to gain experience. I never had a boyfriend during high school, so I thought it would be embarrassing if people found out I was single all my life..." My own words stung. I didn't particularly mind being single during high school, since I felt too young back then anyway, but the loneliness itself was real and I hated voicing its presence.

"Huh." Derek shrugged. "I can understand that, I guess," he said quietly. Only then, after I'd poured out my genuine feelings, did he finally walk away.

Once he was with Cindy again and hopefully cooking up some lie to keep her happy and oblivious, Axel turned his attention back to me and didn't let go of my shoulder.

"So, we're dating?" Axel asked, smiling uncontrollably. I'd just given him the easiest excuse to make fun of me. "Looks like we're going on that date after all."

"*No*. I was just preventing Derek from misunderstanding your reason for being here," I answered, removing his hand from my shoulder once Derek had his back to us. "I had to convince him you weren't planning to steal Cindy away or something." Who knew what he'd do if he got jealous. "We're not going on any dates. In fact, we don't need to see each other *at all* after this."

"That won't convince Derek. Besides, just because we aren't actually dating doesn't mean we can't be friends." He glanced at Cindy, then at the other students passing by. "Have *you* made any friends yet, Zilla?"

"No, I'm only one week in, Axel. Real friendships take time."

That was just an excuse, though. I had already tried to make friends and had been unsuccessful so far. I'd checked out a few of the university's extracurricular groups but no one stood out to me. I was so used to relaxing with Cindy and her chill personality that I wasn't used to small talk. This must be how people in year-long relationships felt after breaking up and trying first dates again. It was exhausting.

"Well, if you ever want to hang out—platonically, that is—I'm always available," Axel offered. "I've never had trouble making friends but understand not everyone has that talent." He grinned at me, not realizing how patronizing he sounded...or maybe he did know and enjoyed rubbing it in. *Or* I was just assuming the worst because I was insecure about my failures. Maybe he really did have pure intentions.

"I'll give you my number," he added, already digging his phone out of his pocket.

I resisted, leaning away and allowing a look of disgust to come over my face. "I really don't want to—"

"You owe me for distracting Derek," he chastised, that relentless smile never leaving his cheeky face.

I continued hesitating but was about to cave and he could tell. He wiggled his phone at me playfully, never ceasing to be entertained by my resistance.

"Fine." Sighing, I held out my own phone and let him put his number there instead. That way, he couldn't start pestering me with texts until I texted him first. Of course, he listed his contact name with hearts on either side, then finally released me.

"Call me!" he shouted as we went our separate ways, him nonchalantly heading back to his friend group and me desperately fleeing. He made a sarcastic phone sign with his fingers as he walked away but I didn't return the gesture.

"What were you talking about with Axel?" Cindy asked me excitedly as I rejoined her and Derek. Derek had taken my spot on the bench so I had to rearrange my backpack and books so I could fit. Cindy waited eagerly as I finally freed enough bench space to sit. I could tell she already assumed Axel and I were close, but it looked like Derek hadn't revealed anything beyond that, just as promised.

"Just asking him why he's here," I said, avoiding her eyes. "He's studying to be an English teacher."

"Small world," Cindy said, which was exactly what Derek said to Axel when he saw him too. She and Derek were starting to sound the same. I'd heard that was what all couples did over time. Cindy and I used to speak similarly in the past, toting the same catch phrases and tone. Now she'd moved on to Derek instead. That hurt a little.

"Yeah." I sighed, relieved that she hadn't become suspicious and Derek didn't look jealous again. I was the only one who understood the bullets we'd just narrowly avoided. Sometimes I wished I wasn't the only one aware that we were puppets on a lame author's string.

No one would ever believe me if I told them, though, so this was my burden to bear alone. "Small world."

Chapter 14

L uckily, Axel didn't interfere in Derek or Cindy's life over the coming days. We barely saw him, since none of our classes overlapped, and after a few weeks, I completely forgot about him. I had other things to worry about, after all, like making friends as I said I would.

Despite my previous school club attempts, I was pretty sure that was where my success would lie, since it was proving difficult to make friends in class. I had to spend the entire one to three hours of class taking notes profusely, then as soon as class ended, everyone headed out the door like the building was on fire. It was so different from high school, where students would normally stay to chat for a bit or loiter in the hallways before heading to their next destination. The intense sense of urgency that came with university life was a total culture shock.

So, clubs were my best bet. They were literally designed to form friendships, after all. The only problem was, there weren't many club subjects that interested me and the ones that did I had already tried and failed at.

I went to a music club on my second day, since I used to play the piano and a little violin, but the people there were so advanced in skill that I felt excluded and left behind.

The second club I went to, Women in Business, should have interested me. I was going into a business, after all, and I was a woman. However, I found it to be a little too focused on the small business and corporate aspect. The club felt like an additional lecture, rather than a place to relax. The women there had already started forming tight-knit groups by the time I walked in too. The cliques I did force my way into and made conversation with were filled with girls who reminded me of the person I was trying to stop being. I felt like if I became friends with them, they'd ruin my goal of becoming less stereotyping and harsh. Since I'd promised myself I would become friends with more laid-back people who weren't too focused on first impressions, I decided that club wasn't the right one for me either.

That left two other possible options. There was a book club, though I already had too many textbooks I needed to read and wasn't fond of adding literature to that pile. Reading books might also remind me of the real-life amateur author constantly peering over my shoulder, and that would get agitating quickly.

That left one final option: the gaming club.

The group members described themselves as both board game and video game enthusiasts. I leaned toward the board games. Video games made me dizzy. But, even if I only played board games, a club like this had to be relaxed and offer an escape from all the studying, right?

So, I decided to try the gaming club. It didn't quite suit my personality, but Axel had encouraged branching out and switching things up, right? So, this might be the exact path I needed.

My heart only sank slightly as I walked into the small, out of place classroom where the gaming club took place. There was one monitor in the corner that was being used to play Mario Cart, along with a couch where the four players were squished together. The rest of the tables were covered in board games. The table closest to me held six students with sheets of paper and dice before them. They must be playing Dungeons and Dragons. The other tables hosted a heated Monopoly game, a deception word game, and something I didn't recognize with a lot of colorful cards involved.

The group was made up of mostly men but there were a few girls at that unknown card table, so I made a beeline for them and sat next to the closest girl: a pretty brunette with short hair and a tattoo across her right eye. I couldn't even tell what it was supposed to depict, but it got the point across that she was both edgy and nerdy.

As soon as that thought crossed my mind, I cringed and remembered what Axel said at graduation. I needed to stop judging based on looks or stereotypes alone. Luckily, as the girl at the head of the table started explaining the rules, I managed to ignore my mental mistake and became more comfortable as the game started. The girls ended up being very sweet and helpful. Some of them were a bit odd, using old-fashioned slang and referencing media I didn't recognize, but they still put me at ease.

Things were going well...until a certain someone walked in and ruined all my plans.

Axel Burns. The author's favorite character, apparently.

Chapter 15

"Who is that?" the tattoo girl whispered, nudging me as though I was going to answer. "He's cute."

I frowned in confusion as all the girls looked past me at someone who had just walked in. Then I heard his voice calling the names of two boys on the couch, and my shoulders slumped. Axel hadn't hung out with gamers in high school. What excuse could the author possibly make to change that now?

I refused to turn around and focused on the girl who just addressed me. "Can you help me with this?" I whispered, showing her my cards. "I'm not sure if I should play the hearts or the jack."

The girl sweetly helped me out, Axel forgotten in her wish to teach me. However, the other girls still snuck occasional glances at Axel as the game continued. I heard him drop onto the couch and start playing but I focused on my own table and those around it. This club was all about meeting *new* people. I already knew Axel, so there was no need to speak to him.

Maybe I should have looked after all, though. Every time I heard Axel's voice, it sent a wave of heat over my chest and made me more nervous than I already was.

I wasn't stupid. I could acknowledge that I was attracted to Axel. That didn't mean I had to like it or respond to it, though.

The rush of emotions didn't go away when he finally spotted me. "Zilla!"

I closed my eyes for a moment, then smiled at the other girls before looking over my shoulder.

Axel waved at me from the couch, flashing an ever-growing smile.

"Hey." I nodded at him, then turned back to my new tattooed friend. "Could you—"

"I wasn't expecting to see you here," Axel said, his controller forgotten as he approached our table. I felt my chances of forming friendships with these new girls slip away as he dragged a nearby chair over and plopped down right beside me. All female eyes were on him now.

"So, what are we playing?" he asked with a cheeky grin, directing it at the girl who had been explaining the rules earlier. This girl, at least, seemed immune to his charms and didn't miss a beat. She summarized her explanation again, then started a new round by tossing out the cards like a professional dealer. I realized why she didn't sneak glances at Axel like a few of the other girls when one of the boys playing Dungeons and Dragons came over and whispered something in her ear. He was probably her boyfriend.

...Must be nice.

Wait. Must be nice? Where did that come from? I'd never *wanted* a boyfriend growing up. I had never once felt jealous of Cindy or any other girl in a relationship. My main source of jealousy came from Derek taking away my best friend. So, what was causing this change in me?

I resisted the urge to steal a look at Axel upon this realization, trying to figure out if he was the cause or if it was just a coincidence.

Then I blushed when I realized sneaking a look at him made me just like the three other girls doing the same.

I bit back the urge to sigh and focused on the table again. Luckily, there were a few others more focused on the game itself than the boy next to me, so it helped me focus.

As the game proceeded and I noticed several of the girls and a lot of the boys address Axel by name, I realized this wasn't Axel's first time in this club. That also meant he'd managed to make a lot more friends than me after only a few weeks. Once again, it stung to acknowledge how he excelled at making friends quickly while I only managed the barest of conversations.

There I was with that jealousy again. I was witnessing so many of my own weaknesses come to light. First my judgmental nature was on display, now my jealousy. Had I always been this way or was Axel just shedding light on it? Cindy was never the type to critique or comment on what I did, so I must have been living with my flaws unchecked for most of my life.

Thanks to Axel, everyone was relaxed and laughing by the end of the fifth round. He was good at keeping games upbeat, especially when he was losing. He was a master of self-deprecating jokes.

However, I was beginning to feel my own mental energy drain. Half of me was glad Axel was here, taking the edge off, but the other half reminded me I was relying on him now, and that might prove to be a barrier to making friends in the future.

In the end, I only spent two hours in the gaming club, then made an excuse about having to meet someone and left. The girls at the table said goodbye and waved, which was nice, but I was sure they were just being polite. Even when the tattooed girl gave me her number, asking to hang out again, my insecurities convinced me none of them actually cared. I mean, who would when Axel was around, right?

The only person who didn't give me these doubts was Axel.

As soon as I got up, he did too and gave an equally lame excuse about needing to leave. Then he followed me out and wouldn't stop trailing me down the halls as I tried to escape into the fresh outdoor air.

He must have noticed my nervousness and was coming to comfort me. That, or he wanted another excuse to bug me. Either way, I was partly grateful and partly wishing he'd leave me be. The first part won out, so I didn't tell him to go away.

"So," he said as he stepped through the building's exit and started following me toward the dorm buildings. "How do you think it went? The girls in that club are really nice. I'm sure they'd love to see you again."

"They're nice to *you*, I'm sure," I said, then bit my lip, annoyed at my biting tone. I was lucky Axel smiled, understanding that my anxiety was making me act up. His eyes stayed warm and sympathetic. I could tell he understood my personality by this point and was pitying me.

"Don't worry," he said quietly. "I won't get in your way next time."

Did he sound…sad? Now I felt guilty. I'd taken out my own problems on him when he'd just been trying to help.

"No, it's fine. You're not in the way, Axel. I'm sorry. You can go—"

"And when I say I'll get out of your way, I mean I'll be playing brawl games like I always do!" he cut in mischievously, changing his tone and leaning forward to catch a glimpse of my reaction. "I don't normally play in the card game section. I just went there today to tease you. How was the club?"

I squinted at him, unable to tell if he was super smart or super stupid. Was he aware of how I felt and trying to help by joking around? Or was he blissfully unaware?

The urge to be sarcastic rose and I gave into it. "Good. You were getting in my way anyway. Plus, you kept losing—"

Axel grinned, eager to counter with even more sarcasm. "And I did it for you. I didn't want you to feel bad for coming dead last," he said.

I rolled my eyes dramatically. "Anyway," I said quietly, shoving my hands into my pockets. "I'm just checking out a variety of clubs. I might stay in this one. I might not. I don't know."

"Oh? What other ones were you thinking of?"

I paused and stared at him. "Are you planning to go to those ones too, just to bug me?" Like when he asked me what university I was going to so he could go there too?

"No, no. I was just curious. Some of my friends attend a variety of clubs so I thought I'd give you a head start on forming a few acquaintances."

"Thanks," I muttered, turning away so I wouldn't have to see his puppy-dog expression. He looked thrilled that I'd genuinely thanked him.

"I'm glad you came," Axel said as we reached the end of the path. We'd have to part ways now, unless he wanted to enter the girls dorm...which he might be totally comfortable doing. "See you next week then?"

"...Sure." I ignored the bubbles floating up in my chest and made sure to keep my expression neutral as we said goodbye. I did want to go back to the club—not just because the girls had been nice but because I liked talking to Axel. Sure, he was a flirt and constantly teased me, but I knew his heart was in the right place, at least when it came to our friendship. I didn't know why he kept doing me favors but I was starting to appreciate it. I might as well accept the invite to return to the club.

Chapter 16

Derek and I shared one class during our first semester. It was a required Asian history class—or rather, one of five history courses we could choose from, and he and I ended up taking the same one by accident. However, since he already had a friend in that class, we didn't sit next to each other. That suited me just fine since I wasn't actually friends with him, and we only saw each other when Cindy was around.

However, my seat on the far left side of the room did offer me a perfect view of his seat...and of a pretty blonde girl who kept looking over at him. It seemed Axel wouldn't be the only blonde rival interfering in my best friend's love story.

I didn't blame the girl for staring over the coming weeks. Like I said, Derek had a Golden Retriever, boy-next-door look about him. While Axel gave off a dangerous, flighty feeling to girls, Derek offered a sense of comfort and loyalty. I wasn't surprised he received at least a few double takes.

However, on the fourth week, the girl sat right in front of him and started asking him for help with her homework. Then she'd ask to copy his notes. Then, before I knew it, she was sitting right next to him and getting too close. Her knee kept bumping into his, her hair started falling onto his shoulder, and she began whispering right into his ear. Seeing it made me uncomfortable for Cindy's sake.

Luckily, it was clear Derek wasn't interested. He would sometimes scoot the chair a little to the right when she got too close, and he didn't look happy about receiving her attention either. Regardless of his reactions, the girl still riled up the protective older sister inside me. I wanted to prevent anyone from getting in Cindy's way or making her feel sad. I knew it was weird to interfere, but it was hard to ignore.

So, after a month of watching these awkward encounters take place, I decided something needed to be done. Wasn't Axel enough of a rival to satisfy the author's needs? We didn't need a second love triangle! I hated those things anyway. They never brought the proper amount of tension but *did* manage to hurt someone's feelings every time.

I refused to let the dumb author have her way (I was just presuming it was a 'she' at this point), so instead of studying that weekend or attending the gaming club, I decided to finally use that phone number Axel had given me weeks ago. It was time to cash in that IOU, or rather, pay it off.

I started by texting him a simple **Hey** to get the conversation rolling. I didn't want to seem eager to talk to him…because I wasn't. Not at all. It wasn't like I enjoyed speaking to him or anything. Well, maybe I did but…Whatever.

Five minutes after I texted him, he replied. He was fast compared to Cindy and especially Derek when it came to responding.

Hey! I've been waiting eagerly for you to text me. What's up?

I hesitated. I really was using him like a tool now, ironically. But I knew he wouldn't get mad at me for asking for help…and I still didn't have a lot of friends to rely on so there was no one else to turn to...

Plus, he was a playboy. Flirting with girls was his trademark, so asking him to flirt with a girl yet again should be easy. Noncommittal relationships were a daily activity for him, after all.

But it was definitely wrong of me to ask this of him. I knew it and already felt bad.

Hey, I typed again. ***Can you come to the history building tomorrow at 12?***

That was when Derek and the blonde chick had class together. I could show the girl to Axel so he knew exactly who to target. Plus, I'd rather explain the situation in person so he wouldn't misunderstand anything.

Sure thing! was his reply.

Man, I felt awful. It sounded like I was scheduling a regular hangout, rather than a nefarious meeting to scheme and sabotage. Would he be disappointed when he found out I was abusing our friendship?

I felt even worse when I met him the next day. I ditched the class so I could meet him in the hallway beside the door, its glass window offering the perfect view of the girl and her proximity to Derek.

Axel looked great as he strolled up, wearing a purple button-down that complimented his eyes. He looked thrilled to see me too, though he gave that bright eyed and pink cheeked look to everyone. It was why he became so popular. He knew how to convince a girl he was seriously interested in her, even when he was just messing around.

"So, what does my girlfriend need from me today? I don't get a single text all month and now she's asking me out? It must be important." He draped his arm around my shoulders and pulled me close, playing up our fake relationship even though there was no one around to see it.

"I need another favor," I said, pulling his arm off as I always did. "With Derek."

"Oh." His entire aura changed, becoming droopy. If Derek was a Golden Retriever, Axel was a Doberman, and they had both mastered the art of looking sad and pitiful when the situation required it. "What do you want me to do?"

I explained the situation quickly, then led a hesitant Axel to the classroom door to show him the girl. She was wearing glasses today and was tapping a pencil on Derek's desk to get his attention.

"So, you want me to pretend to like her?" Axel whispered, sighing after he got a good look and leaning against me like he needed my support. "And you really think that will resolve the situation? It might make things worse."

"It'll work. You're good looking and charismatic. Compared to Derek, I'm sure she wouldn't mind switching her interest over to you. You're single, right? So it shouldn't be a problem." I felt my logic dull as the BFF role took over.

"Yeah. Yeah." He was shaking his head as he said it, though. Was he lying or just disappointed in my reliance on him?

"If you don't want to do this, you can just say no. You don't owe me anything," I said quietly, having second thoughts. I'd never met someone who was so disappointed by me all the time. Axel always managed to make me feel bad about every trait I possessed.

"I just think that you should let Derek and Cindy deal with their problems on their own," he said with another, longer sigh. "They're not children."

"That's true, but they're shy and non-confrontational. They need a little shove in the right direction."

"Derek is not afraid to tell people like it is," Axel countered. "I heard how he spoke to you in the library, remember? If he wanted to tell that girl off, he would have." He sounded a little pissed. For once, I felt like I was hearing his genuine, unfiltered thoughts.

"So, you won't do it?" I kind of wished he would reject me. I was already starting to regret asking him to do this.

"...I will. But..." He pursed his lips and turned away. "This is the last time, Zilla. We're almost twenty. You need to let them live their own lives."

He was right.

"And you also need to start living yours."

What was that supposed to mean?

"I *am* living my own life. It's just...Cindy's life is different from mine. She has different...needs." Main character needs were different from side character needs.

"How?"

I couldn't explain the main and side character roles to him. He wouldn't believe me. It sounded insane, even to me.

Wishing to avoid the subject, I tried to distract him. "Look, if you do this for me, I'll go to the movies with you."

"Deal!" He said it so quick, it almost made me jump. Then his pleased smile made my heart *actually* leap. It was pretty clear he'd been waiting a long time to hear me accept his invitation, though that could either be because he was interested in me *or* because I was a challenge to overcome.

Regardless of his reasoning, at least I'd avoided telling him about my insane theory and seeing him judge me for it.

My acknowledgement of this date confirmed one thing in my mind, though. The author definitely planned to put me and him together. The fact that I'd been unable to come up with a counteroffer proved it. I was normally a pretty innovative thinker when it came to solutions, yet my mind went blank when it came to Axel. The author must have been messing with my brain, pushing me closer to this playboy, and that was a recipe for disaster. I was not the type of girl to date a cheater. Never, in a million years, would I go on a *real* date with him. This was just a fake date—a simulation and business negotiation.

I wasn't letting the author have her way. This was just a means to an end for me. That was all. My stupid heart skipping a beat was just a...biological reaction. Nothing more. The best friend couldn't fall in love with the playboy and come out free of scars. So, I wouldn't fall in love. That was Cindy's job, not mine.

That was what I told myself at least, though my head and heart didn't quite agree.

Chapter 17

Axel's mission to get that girl away from Derek took a little longer this time, but a week after I sent that text, Cindy told me the girl had stopped following Derek around. Derek must have finally told her about it. Well, that was good. I was glad things worked out for them, even if it required a bit of sacrifice on my end.

I went to class the next week and saw the girl sitting at the other end of the room, far away from Derek. She had higher aspirations now. By the time she realized Axel had been playing with her heart, it would be too late, and the semester would be over.

My actions may have hurt her, but...as cruel as it was, I prioritized Cindy over everyone else. Sure, it was selfish, but if I looked at our world as a book revolving around Cindy, it didn't make me feel quite as bad.

The following night, I received a text from Axel.

Top Machete. Friday night. 8PM.

He might be a cheater but at least he was a man of his word when it came to sabotaging stalkers and creating jealousy. I smiled as I replied with a simple **OK** but I planned to pay for our tickets separately, just so he knew this wasn't an actual date.

Friday came around too quickly. After I finished my classes, I spent a full hour trying to figure out what to wear. At first, I thought about wearing something nice, like a navy-blue dress or at least a frilly pink shirt with jeans, but then I reminded myself I should try to discourage both Axel and the author by picking the worst outfit I could muster. When I stood in front of the mirror in a wrinkled t-shirt and long shorts, I realized Axel already knew how I normally dressed. If I went out of my way to look ugly, he'd figure out what I was up to and probably tease me about it. That would just serve as a different, but equally *romantic*, plot point. Sighing, I gave up on either extreme and decided to choose something completely random.

I closed my eyes and spun around with my hand out, pointed in the direction of my small dorm closet. My extremely careful and precise wardrobe management resulted in a pair of black jeans with a red plaid button-up and white sneakers. It ended up looking cute, which made me both relieved and annoyed. Part of me wanted to look nice for Axel, but I had to remind myself I should be doing the opposite.

Anyway, Axel was used to dating girls with much nicer wardrobes, so there was zero chance of him being impressed regardless of what I chose. It really didn't matter what I did so I should stop overthinking this.

I arrived at the movie theater outside our university campus five minutes early, treating this date like a normal class. The building was tall and dark but the lights inside and glowing posters lining the wall made it less intimidating. Axel was already waiting outside the door, studying some superhero movie posters on the wall. How early had he arrived? Did he do it in an attempt to impress me?

"Ah yes, Scorpion Man," I commented as I walked up behind him, pointing at the poster. "Your favorite superhero? He looks a little...uh..."

"Hey, don't knock the Scorpion. His stinger can paralyze you in seconds," Axel said, turning on me with a huge grin. He was wearing black jeans, just like me, and a crimson t-shirt that showed off his arms. His hair looked nice too, though I couldn't quite put my finger on why. I hated how good-looking he was. If only that face could be attached to a boy I could actually date.

"You look nice," he added, leading me inside. His hand hovered behind my back but he never tried to touch me. I must have removed his hands enough times that he'd learned his lesson.

He was about to pay for the tickets but I insisted on paying for my own, then I did the same for the drink. Axel didn't look surprised. He even smirked, which made me wonder if I was being too predictable and playing into the side character stereotype too much.

"So, how did you do it?" I asked as we entered a mostly empty theater and sat at the back. An ad for popcorn played, displaying the kernels riding a rollercoaster toward a vat of butter where they would probably die.

"Do what?" he asked. "Find the emptiest theater in the city even though this is the best-selling movie this month?"

"You know what I'm talking about," I muttered with a chuckle, ignoring the second dumb ad, which advertised the drink I'd already bought. Why would the author bother to advertise something we already had? "How'd you convince that girl to leave Derek alone?"

"Same thing I'm doing right now," he said, popping a kernel into his mouth. "I took her to watch Top Machete."

"Seriously?" He'd put more work into this than I expected.

"Yup. Now I get to watch it again and see what I missed during my bathroom break last time."

"Wow. You really know how to make a girl feel special," I said. How generous of him to take me to the same thing.

"Hey, now." He laughed, tilting his head toward the ceiling as he chuckled. I couldn't be sure if that movement meant it was a real laugh or a fake one. I'd seen him do it plenty of times before. "Last time was a mission, so I couldn't relax. Now I'm here purely for fun so I'll get to actually focus on the movie."

That felt surprisingly hurtful because it meant he didn't plan to pay attention to me, but it was also a relief because it meant he was viewing this as a friendship event instead of a date.

The film started and we stopped chatting so Axel could focus, though he did drape both arms over the tops of the seats, causing his wrist to brush up against my back.

As we sat there, I realized part of me wished he *would* pay attention to me. What a stupid wish. I should be relieved he viewed me as a friend. I didn't want to wind up like all the other girls he broke the hearts of.

But the slight sting in my heart remained. If only this stupid organ could get the memo that my brain had a long time ago. Axel Burns was bad news. My role was to take advantage of him and come out unscathed. I was supposed to be too smart to fall for him.

Chapter 18

"I'm actually surprised by how much I enjoyed that," I admitted as we exited the theater together. We had just finished the film and I only needed two bathroom breaks throughout. I shouldn't have ordered a soda after all.

There was always something special about watching a movie in the theater that made me leave with a weird high. "Who knew tanks could actually make for an emotional story?"

"Right?" Axel asked cheerfully, quite pleased with himself. Ten minutes into the film, I'd felt and acted disinterested, but by the end, I was leaning forward in my seat, completely invested.

As we walked out and a cold breeze blew over us, Axel smoothly draped his coat over my shoulders without asking for permission.

"I think I saw you crying too," Axel added, grinning cheekily.

"I was not!"

"You totally were."

"Well, you were the one who got teary-eyed at the romance scene," I countered, poking him in the chest. "And it wasn't even a sad one."

"Reunited love always brings a tear to my eye," he defended, his face scrunching up in a mock sob. "So, you want to get a drink or something?"

"Um, last I checked, we weren't 21 yet, Axel."

"I wasn't talking about alcohol, you weirdo; although we *can* technically drink at nineteen in Ontario."

"Doesn't matter. We're still eighteen." And my point still stood. I wasn't in the mood to drink, especially with him.

"I was referring to a milkshake or something," he countered. "I know you went to the bathroom three times during the movie but—"

"You are just *begging* for me to walk away right now," I warned good-naturedly, unable to prevent myself from smiling at his laid-back teasing. This made me wish I had more guy friends growing up. It was fun to joke around with Axel, though I couldn't say the same for Derek. "But sure, why not? I am feeling hungry since I didn't get any of that popcorn. You ate it all before the trailers ended."

"I'm a tall guy. I require sustenance."

I raised an eyebrow, making a show of being unimpressed but not countering him. Despite approaching adulthood, he was still growing a few inches every year.

"Okay, there's a restaurant right around the corner," Axel said. "We can pop over for a quick bite. I'll buy you a snack and—"

"I will buy *myself* a snack because this is *not* a date."

He pretended to be shocked. "It's not?"

"No. It's not."

"But that's what you agreed to. If this isn't a date, you still owe me one." He grinned, knowing he'd just tricked me and I'd walked right into it. "There's a Rodent Man movie coming out next week. Why don't we go there next Friday and this time—"

"Nope. I lied. This *was* a date," I said, adding punctuation mark signs with my fingers to emphasize it. "So you can take some other girl to see Rodent Man. I'm sure any woman would be thrilled to receive the invitation."

"Why ask another girl when I have *you* right here?"

"Don't bother flattering me, Mr. Playboy Rival. I'm not easy like all the other girls you go on dates with."

Axel raised an eyebrow. "First of all, that's rude to all the other girls. Secondly, Mr. Playboy Rival?"

Shoot! I accidentally used the book labels. He'd made me way too comfortable and I'd let it slip. "It's...nothing." I turned away, cringing and hurrying down the sidewalk toward the restaurant. I'd rather escape back to my dorm, but I'd already agreed to the drink and felt like I'd ruin the deal if I broke my word again.

"No, hold on. We need to talk about this. This isn't the first time you've done this." He stopped walking and wouldn't continue until I rejoined him. "Is that really how you see me? As a playboy? And a rival on top of it? A rival for who?"

Phew. He wasn't suspicious about the book terms...I mean, why would he be? It wasn't normal to think the way I did.

When I didn't say anything, he prodded me again. "I've been meaning to ask you about this for a while. It's weird when you bring up labels like that. Sometimes you act like you're the main character of the world or something."

So he did notice after all. Dang it. "That's just something I do for fun," I lied, speeding up again to get away from him. "And besides, if the world revolved around someone, it wouldn't be me because I am *not* the main character."

"Why not?" he laughed, easily keeping pace with me.

"Because protagonists have to either be super good looking so everyone loves them against their will, or super plain, though all the guys around her end up falling for her anyway."

"Super plain? That's extremely specific—Wait." He snapped his fingers. "I see where this is going. You're talking about Cindy, aren't you?"

"Yes, I am." Huh. He wasn't as dumb as I first thought...Actually, he'd never once acted dumb around me, not unless he was pretending so he could get a rise out of me. "You should be agreeing with me. You fell for her after bumping into her in the hallway, remember? So did Derek and Tom Spencer and Nathaniel Stevens in high school. Oh, and she was asked out by two different guys in her Linguistics class just this month." I sighed when I realized I was rambling. What's worse, it made me look jealous of Cindy. I wasn't. I just didn't like how absurd the situation was.

Axel was just listening with a smile pasted on his face. I could tell he was having fun listening to this dumb stuff. It was ammo for more teasing later.

"Well, you can't lump me in with those guys. If I was like them, we wouldn't be having this conversation right now," he said when I finally stopped talking. "I flirt with everyone equally. That way, no one's feelings get hurt."

"I don't agree with that," I grumbled, grabbing the door handle of the restaurant to let myself in. "Flirting is supposed to make someone feel special. Doing it to everyone defeats the purpose," I countered.

I stepped inside but he didn't follow. Had I said something to bother him again?

I turned around and saw him standing in the doorway, forehead wrinkled slightly. He was thinking over what I'd said and looked conflicted.

"Should we not get food after all?" I asked, aware I'd rustled his feathers but not regretting what I said. I'd meant it.

"No, no." He shook his head and followed me. "Let's just…change the subject for now, okay?"

"Okay," I said quietly as we entered the small, blue-walled restaurant. It smelled of grease and salt. I brushed off one of the tables on my way to the counter.

"Good," Axel said. As I watched the restaurant workers deal with the drive thru customers, I saw my "date" shift back to his normal self, no longer thinking about what I'd said. Maybe he'd shelved that comment for later. "Look, regardless of us being polar opposites and disagreeing on some things, I think we should just acknowledge," Axel paused as I ordered some fries, "that this date is the perfect in-between. The guy who treats everyone the same is going on a special date with a special girl—"

"You said earlier that it *wasn't* special. You took that other girl to Top Machete too—"

"Meanwhile, the girl who never gives anyone attention is out on a date with a guy like me." Axel didn't skip a beat, completely ignoring my snarky interruption. "This is a match made in heaven. Opposites attract, right?"

"That applies to magnets, not people," I said, wanting to laugh and roll my eyes at the same time. I'd heard in psychology class that couples with similar personalities actually got along better in the long run.

"Seriously though, back to that weird statement from before," Axel said as we sat down with our food. He had ordered a soda and milkshake, though he kept pushing both toward me, and I had ordered fries to make up for the missed popcorn. "The playboy bit I get, but rival? Seriously?"

I shoved a fry in my mouth to avoid answering the question for a bit but, sadly, he was a patient man. "Yes, you're a rival. For...Derek..."

"Derek?" He laughed a deep, hearty laugh that I rarely heard him use. His normal laugh was a bit higher and subdued. Just as I thought, the one he used when lifting his head toward the ceiling was fake after all. Only now was he showing his genuine, more silly side. "Are you talking about when I asked Cindy out to prom that one time? They weren't on speaking terms back then. I don't count that as a rivalry at all."

"Well, I do."

"Okay. Well, that was—"

"Look, if you really want to know the reason, it's because...I..." I might regret revealing this but he kept nagging me about it so it was time to just admit the truth. "The truth is, Axel, that...I think we're living in a book and...Cindy is...the main character..." I paused. "Aaand you're looking at me like I'm crazy."

"Yes, I am, because that *is* crazy." He laughed again, then it shifted into a concerned chuckle. "Wait. You're serious, aren't you?"

"Look." I leaned forward, lowering my voice. "I'm not insane or anything, okay? There are just so many coincidences happening around her that I'm beginning to take the theory seriously."

"Okay. I'll humor you." He leaned back in his seat so we were in opposite poses. "What are these coincidences?"

"Well..." I paused to get things straight in my head. "First of all, I am the complete definition of the cliché best friend who doesn't have a boyfriend, offers advice, and doesn't get in the way of her best friend's love life."

He tilted his head sideways, one side of his mouth quirked up in an 'I disagree but won't counter you just yet' look.

"And Cindy is the exact stereotype of a plain, relatable, quiet girl who all the guys fall for. Plus, she kept having super coincidental encounters with Derek. They fell on top of each other and accidentally kissed, things kept breaking around them that made them get closer, then when their relationship needed a little shove, you showed up to be a rival. After your role was done, you immediately backed out of the picture so Derek could comfort her. It was all a bit too perfect."

"Aha!" He stopped me. "That's wrong! I didn't back out. *You* prevented me from chasing after Cindy because you wanted to give them some alone time. That was *your* fault, not the universe's."

"I did it because the plot demanded it!"

"So, the fact is that we aren't living in a book. You're just interfering to make it fit this plot you imagined. You're the one creating those coincidences!"

"Look, Axel, I don't care if you believe me—"

"I believe that *you* believe it, but if we're just characters living at an author's every whim, why are you and I meeting right now?" he said and hesitated, trying to figure out if I was angry at him or not. I was, a little. I didn't blame him, though. The coincidences had died down lately...but I had an explanation for that.

"I'll tell you why. The writer is trying to create some new contrived plot where *I* fall in love with you, then you break my heart and it creates a little drama but doesn't interfere with the happy ending for the main characters."

It felt a little satisfying to finally get this off my chest.

I was expecting Axel to laugh at everything I said, or at least counter it again and make some joke at my expense. But instead, his eyes lit up even though his smile disappeared. "The writer wants to make you fall for me?" He paused so I could let that sink in, then asked, "*Are* you in love with me, Zilla?"

"No," I insisted, so quickly it made me look like a liar. His smug look told me he thought the same.

"No," I repeated adamantly. "Like I said, I'm not into playboys." I might find him attractive and like his laugh and appreciate how he kept helping me...but that didn't mean I wanted to date him.

"Well, Miss Xiang, I hate to break it to you but if we dated, I think *you* would be the one dumping me, not the other way around."

"Uh huh. Because you'd cheat on me?"

"No." He finally sat up and leaned forward so he was invading my personal space again. "Because you would overthink things and fall into the miscommunication trope." He raised his eyebrows, looking proud for using book terms. "You'd probably convince yourself I didn't love you and not realize you were wrong until it was too late. After that happened, you would chase me down in an airport and run into my open arms." He stretched his hands out wide, looking ready to burst out laughing as he did so. "Just like in the movies."

I scoffed, a bit too loudly. "Yeah, right. That seems a little unrealistic."

"I thought we were in a book," he said, gesturing to our surroundings. "If we are, the airport reunion makes perfect sense."

"Sure, it could happen," I conceded, "*if* I was the main character, but I'm *not*. I'm the side character, which means I get the realistic ending where you pretend to love me, then you eventually get bored and find some other girl."

"That's a little unfair. I've been with plenty of other girls, but I've never been in love," he defended himself, "So you can't accuse me of leaving a *loving* relationship when I've never been in one before."

After he said that, he looked at me with those stupid dreamy eyes, telling me I could be that special someone. I hated how it felt like a scene in a movie. I also hated how it sent heat rushing into my chest.

"If you and I got together, things would be different," he added quietly.

"Nope. Stop that." I pressed my finger against his forehead and pushed him back in his seat. This wouldn't work on me, not in a book or in real life. "I'm not falling for that. Have you ever thought about your name, Axel, and how it's the most cliché, jock, playboy name? That's because you fit the—"

"Were you drinking alcohol during those bathroom breaks?" he interrupted. "Because unless my ears deceived me, I just confessed my love to you and you're still talking about book tropes."

What was he talking about? "Because you're the type of guy to say that to anyone—"

"If I kissed you, would you finally believe me?"

I took a deep breath, forcing myself to say, "Nope. I've seen you making out with girls in the library while dating someone else. Kissing doesn't translate to 'I love you' in your language."

"You're talking about the girlfriend I wasn't actually serious about. She wasn't that into me either. She just wanted to date me because I was 'hot and sexy' in her words."

"You still cheated."

"And you'd be different."

"I would not." That was what cheaters always said.

Axel squinted at me.

Okay, I could tell he'd had enough of the bickering. He crossed him arms and sat back in his chair. "Okay. What do I need to do to convince you to date me?"

Was he being serious? He couldn't be—

His eyes told me otherwise.

This must be the author's doing. How had we transitioned from me talking about the book we lived in, to him genuinely asking me out? I felt like I'd just missed a crucial step in this conversation. This couldn't be real.

"Nothing. There's nothing you can do to convince me," I said quickly. I was not falling for his or the author's stupid game! I wasn't a pawn to be played with and dumped.

No longer caring if I looked rude, I packed up my bag, left my fries on the table, and headed for the door. "Thanks for the movie, Axel. Good luck on the next date with Mouse Man."

"Rodent Man," he corrected quietly. He didn't look annoyed as I headed out the door. He just seemed sad...or regretful.

Dang it, now I felt bad *again*. How many times had he done that to me now? He always made me question everything about myself and left me feeling guilty as I walked away from him. Sure, sometimes he was right about me but...

My heart stung as I walked down the dark, empty street toward the dorm I shared with Cindy. This pain in my chest was probably just a reaction to being criticized by him. I wasn't in love. This wasn't even a crush. I refused to fall for a guy like him.

Luckily, we didn't share any classes, so there was no chance of running into him again. I could put this experience behind me and move on. These feelings inside me would simmer down eventually. I just had to wait.

Chapter 19

"So, Zilla, what's Axel up to these days?" Derek asked from across the cafeteria table. He was seated next to Cindy, his arm draped protectively around her shoulder. His voice was nearly blocked out by the chatter and clinking of silverware around them. I had to lean forward to hear him. Cindy had been focused on a romance novel throughout the meal, but her head shot up as soon as he brought up Axel.

"Axel?" I tried to feign ignorance. "How should I know? It's not like I talk to him every day."

Cindy glanced at Derek, raising her eyebrows, then looked back at me. "There's no point lying to us. Derek told me you two were dating."

I glared at Derek. He was supposed to keep that a secret. I bristled at the thought that he might have told Cindy because he had some ulterior motive. Maybe he wanted me to stop third wheeling and knew telling Cindy about Axel would force me to spend less time with her. Or perhaps he knew I was lying and wanted to hear me admit it.

…Or maybe I was reading into things too much.

"Did you two break up already?" Derek asked, then lowered his chin slightly. "Or were you lying about your relationship?"

No, I definitely wasn't reading too much into it. Ever since we moved to Canada, I'd gotten a sneaking suspicion that Derek didn't particularly like me. I wasn't sure why. It could just be my paranoia talking. However, despite him being the male lead—which meant he could do no wrong—I still felt uncomfortable around him.

To hide the fact that I was panicking, I took a long sip of water to get my thoughts together. If I said we broke up, I could avoid bringing up Axel again, but judging by Derek's reaction to Axel, he might start getting jealous again, worrying Axel had set his sights back on Cindy. To add to that fact, it would give the author an excuse to create a love triangle for the third time. That simply wouldn't do.

But if I said we *were* still dating, I'd have to bring Axel back into my life and pretend I loved him. We hadn't spoken since that date a week ago. I really didn't want to see him again and was sure the feeling was mutual.

I had a third option available to me, of course. All I had to do was admit I was lying. However, that came with a whole different set of pitfalls. I wouldn't want to disappoint Cindy. She knew I wasn't the type to lie, and this might break her trust in me. Plus, it would give Derek a legitimate excuse to dislike me, and he might use that to turn Cindy against me.

None of these options were ideal, but there was a definite lesser of the three evils.

"We're still dating," I blurted, then froze as I realized what I'd just done. What kind of thought process was that? Out of all three options, saying we *broke up* was the most logical. Why had I said we were still together? It had already been established that Axel never dated girls longer than two months. Breaking up would have been totally believable. Why had I been so stupid? Claiming we were still dating was going to lead to even more misunderstandings down the road!

...

Wait!

Wait, wait, wait!

I knew what was happening here. The author had gotten into my head, forcing me to choose the option she wanted. She didn't care about what was logical, so long as it led toward her objective: making me and Axel date for real (and inevitably break up).

Nooooo! I'd fallen right into her hands and couldn't take it back!

"Oh, good, because I invited him to join us for lunch tomorrow," Derek said, making me glare at him again and try to figure out his motives. Why did he invite Axel? They weren't friends anymore. How would this benefit him? Was it really my third wheeling that was causing all this tension?

I turned my gaze toward Cindy. She looked elated.

I stopped frowning. Why shouldn't she be happy? Her best friend had a boyfriend now. We could go on double dates, and I could stop being the plus one awkwardly tagging along. She'd probably felt sorry for me this whole time. The fact that my supposed boyfriend was Axel Burns, the boy she rejected in high school, didn't appear to have crossed her mind.

"I'm so glad you finally got a boyfriend," she told me sweetly, zero malice in her tone. She had probably dreamed of this day ever since middle school. Cindy always was the more romantic one.

"Great," I said, biting back a sigh. "Thanks, Derek. I'm sure Axel will be thrilled that you invited him."

Chapter 20

"**S**o, Axel, when did you two become close? Zilla never told me the whole story," Cindy prodded as soon as Axel joined us for lunch the next day. Judging by his laidback, elated expression, he didn't bear any ill-will toward me for our "date" a week ago. He also didn't plan to spill the beans about my lie, which was good but would have saved me a lot of trouble down the line.

"Well, we officially met in the cafeteria, as you know, and then again on the night of prom," he said, sitting right next to me. Our knees were nearly touching. "Then we just kept running into each other." I tensed as he wrapped his around me like Derek always did with Cindy, though he did it gently, attempting to make me comfortable rather than shelter or possess me.

"And when did you fall in love with her?" Cindy continued, making me choke on my ice water.

"Well, we—" Axel began but I cut him off by stomping on his foot with my heel. I didn't want to genuinely hurt him. I just wanted him to know that topic was off limits. We shouldn't pile on too many lies.

"Axel," I hissed, shooting him a warning glare. He looked ready to totally lie about my love for him and enjoy every second of it.

Axel wiggled his eyebrows at me, then gave a nod and wink. "We haven't been officially dating for too long so I wouldn't put any labels on my feelings yet," he said. "By the way, how did you hear about our relationship?"

"Derek told me," Cindy said quietly, making me turn a very unhappy look toward her boyfriend again. Derek looked away, taking a sip of 7up as he did.

"And you've been loyal to her?" Cindy added, raising her eyebrows at me. "Zilla isn't the type to tolerate cheaters."

"Why does everyone assume I cheat?" Axel threw his hands in the air dramatically. "I would never cheat in a serious relationship."

"Then that means you've never been in one," I mumbled under my breath. He had cheated plenty of times.

"I heard that," he whispered in my ear, then smiled widely at Cindy. "Don't get her overthinking things, Cindy. Zilla tends to do that," he warned. "It took a long time to convince her to date me. Don't give her any excuses to leave me now."

"I won't," Cindy said, giggling and shooting me a silly look that I didn't return. She thought I'd fallen for the guy. I could tell. She was getting all starry-eyed; the hopeless romantic. *The serious grump falling for the charming playboy.* I was sure Cindy had watched plenty of films with that plot and absolutely adored every one.

The conversation took a more casual turn as the lunch progressed, thanks to Axel and his ability to turn any bland topic into a ten-minute chat. Even Derek joined in after a while. The smooth, laidback vibe Axel brought to the group once again made me rethink my supposed dislike of the guy. He wasn't that bad to talk to when he wasn't attempting to flirt. He was genuinely funny.

"Since you brought up dates, though," Axel said, cutting off his own sentence, "I've been meaning to invite you guys on a double date to the carnival next week. I've wanted to go ever since we moved here and it's ending this month."

"Oh, that sounds great," I said, pretending to be excited. "I'll invite my study buddies too. They'd love to come."

He shot me an 'it's not a double date if you invite more people' look but didn't say anything because Cindy immediately said yes and looked thrilled about it, which meant there was no way for me to say no now. Cindy didn't go out to group events often so this would be good for her.

Great. Now we were going on yet another date, except this one was official.

Later that day, after I fled the scene and found myself in my dorm, I received a text from Axel. He didn't text me too often and when he did it was usually to ask me about my day. I would always reply with one-word answers, so I understood why he rarely messaged me.

What gender are your study buddies?

That was a weird question.

…They're girls. Why? Are you planning to hit on them?

Nope.

And that was all he said. There were ten minutes of silence, then he texted again. *After our date last week, I thought you'd never want to see me again. What gives?*

It wasn't my doing. Derek was the one who invited you to lunch. I think he was trying to get me to admit that I lied to Cindy. I sighed audibly. *I think he has it out for me.*

I think he has it out for you too.

Seriously? So it wasn't just me! *What makes you say that?*

Well, judging by how he talks to you. At first, I thought you were the one being overbearing, which was true at the time, but now you've backed off and he's still being…I don't know. Mean, I guess?

I waited for him to continue. When he didn't, I decided to change subjects and make something clear. *Just so you know, after this date, I think we should "break up".*

Let me guess. "It's not me, it's you?"

I don't want to keep lying to Cindy.

Then why didn't you just tell her we broke up earlier?

Not even *I* had the real answer to that. Well, I did but he didn't believe me about the author thing.

But then again, I'd already told him about the book so there was no point avoiding it now. His impression of me couldn't get any worse. *I think the author was messing with my head. She made me keep the lie going.*

Sounds like an excuse to keep dating me.

I resisted the urge to chuck the phone across the room. He could be so infuriating, yet he only acted that way with me. In books, that was the tell-tale sign that the guy liked the girl, but in real life it just meant he got a thrill out of annoying me. I was too easy to piss off.

We're breaking up after the carnival. End of story.

… … … If that's what you want.

Don't give me those dots. You're making me sound like the bad guy.

There was a two-minute pause, then he replied. *We can still be friends, right?*

…Sure. But I didn't plan to hang out again outside the gaming club. There was only so much inner turmoil I could put up with.

Chapter 21

J ust like the last "date", I spent another hour choosing my outfit before landing on a blue jean jacket and red pants. At the start of that hour, I had convinced myself I didn't care what any of my friends thought, especially Axel, but by the end of that hour, I knew I was lying to myself.

I arrived at the carnival with Cindy and my two other friends, Leandri and Tammy from camp, in tow. The location's entrance was filled with blasting country music and the stink of petting zoo animals. As soon as we reached the front gate and spotted the crowd of people who would be accompanying us, I understood why Axel asked me what gender my friends were.

He was standing there—waiting for us in a crimson t-shirt and blue jeans that matched my outfit almost perfectly—and beside him were two good-looking guys. They were both fairly tall and fit, though their faces didn't stand out as much as Axel's.

I bit back a sigh as I realized what he had done. Axel had just turned this group event into a quadruple date. Whereas before I could hang out with my friends and avoid Axel, now we would inevitably end up in pairs. I would end up with Axel, just the way he wanted.

Very sneaky.

This left me two options. Either go with Axel and play right into the author's hands or pursue one of the other guys beside him and avoid Axel's scheme. Granted, Axel was clearly the best of the three, just going off of looks and charisma alone, but I wasn't supposed to put people in boxes, right? Who knew? Maybe these other guys were really fun to hang out with too.

"Well, Derek's on his way so why don't you three join Axel and his friends while I wait for Derek in the parking lot?" Cindy asked, her face bright from excitement. This was her first carnival. She'd never seen a real Ferris wheel before.

"Great idea." Excitable Tammy grabbed me by the arm and pulled me close. "That dark-haired one is cute. You mind if we break off into couples?"

"Of course not," I said. *I did* mind but I had zero plans of spoiling her fun. "I can go with—"

"I'm really into freckles," Leandri whispered, pointing at the red-haired boy on Axel's right before I could snag him.

"Great." I sighed and raised my hands in defeat. Were these girls crazy? Normally, they'd be fighting over Axel. The author was making them act illogical just so she could set up Axel and me. "I guess we'll meet up later then...stupid author." I muttered the last part under my breath.

Five minutes later, it was just me and Axel on our way to the nearest roller coaster. We left Cindy alone in the parking lot, though I was hesitant to do so, and the other two were more than happy to head toward opposite ends of the park so no one could interrupt their attempts to land a cute boyfriend. Both of them had broken up with their partners during the transition to university, so it made sense for them to be on the lookout for someone new.

"Funny how that worked out," Axel said, looking pleased with himself as we got into a line that claimed it had a thirty-minute wait. I wasn't sure how reliable that estimate was.

"Yeah. Real funny. You see what I mean about this being a book world?" I asked, pointing at our surroundings. "You were the best-looking out of the three and they still went for the other guys!"

"Thank you for the compliment." He angled his head toward me so I could receive the perfect view of his "best-looking" face. "But you're being a little harsh. My friends are great too."

I didn't deny it and studied the vending machine next to the line to end the conversation. Five dollars for a water bottle? They had to be joking.

"Be honest. On a scale of one to ten, how attractive do you really think I am?" Axel asked, still joshing me. His hand was hovering close to mine, so I had to stay one step ahead of him in line to prevent him from draping it over my shoulder.

He was a ten and he knew it. Meanwhile, I was a solid six—maybe a seven if I put on a lot of makeup and curled my hair, which took 45 minutes minimum and had no guarantee of staying curled for longer than two hours. "Axel, I want to just treat this as a fun event and nothing more. Don't bring dating or superficial looks into this, okay?" For once, it would be nice to just act like normal people in a real, logical world without book tropes or cliché situations.

"Okay. Okay. Let's just relax." He agreed. "You're right. I'll stop bringing it up...unless an opportunity arises to make fun of you."

"Of course."

"Hey, don't roll your eyes. I can act normal. Besides, I'll have fun with you either way, dating or not."

"Oy. What did I just say?" I pointed at him accusingly. "No flirting or teasing. You just agreed."

He laughed. "That wasn't flirting. I was just being honest. If I do end up accidentally complimenting you, I deeply apologize from the bottom of my heart."

Why did he enjoy spending time with me? I wasn't fun to be around. I treated him like dirt half the time. "Okay."

"Okay...So I can't hold your hand?"

"Nope." I smirked, feeling I was part of an inside joke now. I rarely got to take part in those.

Once again, I was realizing just how much fun Axel was to be with, especially when the jokes weren't at my expense. I should try rolling with this today and make our outing fun, rather than pushing back against him constantly. That way he'd actually have a genuine reason to enjoy my company and I wouldn't have to wonder why he put so much effort into hanging out with me.

Plus, I was sure the author loved when we bickered—the good old "enemies to lovers" thing—so if she saw us actually getting along as platonic friends, maybe she'd back off.

Chapter 22

I had a ton of fun with Axel, only slightly against my own will. Hanging out with him was a real blast when he was just acting like a normal person and not fitting into the playboy stereotype I always assumed he belonged to. We went on rides, discovered Axel hated riding upside down and was a little claustrophobic, bought cotton candy and chicken fingers, competed in a shooting game which we both lost somehow, and finally went on the Ferris wheel together.

It wasn't long before I realized this was the reason carnivals always appeared in romance novels. In a Ferris wheel, the couple is stuck together, inches apart, and close enough to kiss. They're high above everyone else too, with a perfect view of the city skyline. It's both private and not private at the same time.

It carried a certain thrill that was perfect for a slow-burn love story.

The little rising car was the perfect place to force a romantic encounter while still having a sudden interruption occur that could delay the romance just a little longer.

"I know that look." Axel interrupted my thoughts as I studied the interior of the slightly wobbly Ferris wheel box. "You're worrying about the book thing again, aren't you? Stop that!"

"Sorry. Sorry." I waved my hands around my head, dismissing the thoughts. "We promised not to do that. I know."

He grinned, leaning toward me but in an amused way rather than a flirtatious one. "But you're right. We *are* surrounded by coincidences. I concede on that point."

"Right?" I laughed, glad someone was finally joining in on the wild theory.

He chuckled, staring at me with an imperfect, goofy smile on his face.

Then the Ferris wheel capsule started to wobble and the moment was ruined as he grabbed the railing in a panic. I was tempted to tease him, like I had earlier when he got scared of going upside down on the roller coaster, but I decided against it. He'd had enough humiliation for one day. Instead, I tried to console him by patting his back stiffly, assuring him we were almost done.

"Thanks," he muttered before heaving and looking ready to vomit. After gagging a few times, he decided the floor was more stable than the seats and sat there instead, running a hand through his hair. "You really would make a good nurse," he added as I collapsed next to him so he wouldn't be alone.

"We'll go buy some overpriced water once we're back on solid ground," I told him, keeping a hand on his shoulder to be as comforting as I could. All worries about keeping us apart left my mind. He was a patient in need now.

Axel opened his mouth to say something else, then grinned sheepishly and thought better of it. "That's really nice of you, Zilla."

I frowned, tempted to tease him back now that I had the upper hand. "You're thinking this is out of character for me, aren't you?"

"What is?" he asked, though I could tell he already knew what I was talking about.

"Being nice to you."

"Nah." He shook his head, then paled and gagged again from the dizziness it caused. "Shouldn't have moved my head." He took another deep breath, then continued. "No, I always knew you were a nice person. This is just the first time you've directed it toward me is all." And his entire countenance had brightened from it, despite looking ready to vomit at the same time. "It's nice."

"Well." I turned away, knowing the top of my cheeks were turning pink. "I'll try to do it more from now on."

We were nearly back on solid ground when my phone started buzzing. I had to take it because it was so rare for me to receive a phone call. I figured it had to be something important.

I was even more surprised to find that it was Derek calling. He never called me, except to schedule something for Cindy.

"Derek?" I asked, nervous. "What's wrong?"

Axel helped me off the Ferris wheel when the ride ended even though he was the one in need of assistance. He stayed quiet so I could hear the call.

"It's Cindy," Derek's panicked voice said over the cell, snapping me out of my sappy thoughts and into the present. "She was with me a few minutes ago, then I went to the bathroom and when I came back, she was gone."

I felt my entire body go cold and could tell by Axel's expression that I must look horrified. "Okay. Did she say anything? Maybe she went to the bathroom too?"

"I waited for five minutes. She's not here!"

"Okay. Calm down. Start searching for her and I'll look too. I'll call her cell after you hang up." Before I could say more or even tell him goodbye, he hung up on me.

"What's wrong?" Axel whispered as I pulled him through the crowd, already scanning every brunette's face for Cindy's. Axel and I were holding hands now, but it wasn't as romantic as I wanted my first hand-holding experience to be. My palms were sweaty and I was freaking out.

"Cindy's missing and I'm worried it might be related to some traumatic experience that always happens in books," I nearly shouted, already pressing Cindy's contact name on the cell phone to call her. It rang five times, then went to voicemail. "Dang it!" Even ignoring the main character aspect, she could have been attacked or kidnapped. Cindy wasn't a strong girl, and she might be too meek to fight back or call out for help. I'd bet she wouldn't even scream if someone grabbed her.

"She'll be fine," Axel told me quietly, peering over people's heads to search for her. "We can find the person who makes announcements and ask them to help us."

"*You* can do that. I need to find her now! She's probably been stolen or is getting hit on by men who can't take no for an answer!" It was such a common trope and would scare her so much she might never go out in public again!

"I'm not leaving you." He gripped my hand, preventing me from running off. "Take a deep breath, Zilla. You're hyperventilating."

Yes, I totally was. It felt like I was drowning. I was sucking in air but nothing was getting to my lungs. My head was turning fuzzy too, dulling my racing thoughts.

His hands were cool as they gripped my shoulders and I took five deep breaths. Then my head calmed, and I had a clear enough mind to hear Derek's voice shouting from a few feet away. Axel heard it too. We both turned, white-faced and wide-eyed, and beheld the most awful, stereotypical sight in the plot so far.

Derek was beating the crap out of two guys. It looked like something out of a thriller.

Chapter 23

The first person I spotted was Cindy, who was crouching against the wall of a food stand with her hands over her head. Her eyes were shut and her lips pressed tight, her body frozen in fear.

Next, my eyes trailed toward two young men a few feet away from her. One was on the ground getting kicked in the stomach, and the other was shouting weakly for Derek leave his buddy alone. I didn't recognize either of them and they didn't seem to know Derek or Cindy either.

Axel squeezed my hand, then pushed me away from the fight. "Stay here. I'll deal with this."

My mind went blank as Axel tried to step between Derek and his victim, trying to prevent any more kicks or punches from being thrown.

This wasn't how the story was supposed to go. Derek was supposed to land one punch to avenge his victimized girlfriend, then check on Cindy to see if she was okay. That was it.

Male leads were only supposed to use violence sparingly (unless the author couldn't tell the difference between abuse and protection). Instead, Derek was laying into the guy, bloodying his face and definitely breaking a rib with his boots. He didn't even stop when Axel grabbed his arm.

When Derek turned around and punched Axel in the face too—his face red from bloodthirst—I screamed for a security guard to come help. This was getting out of hand. My first thought was that Axel's face was too handsome to get punched. The second was that maybe I should grab a weapon and join in before Derek ended up hurting Cindy, who was still crouching a few feet away. I didn't believe Derek would physically hurt her, but he might accidentally do it by swinging too wide.

Luckily, Derek stopped after I shouted. As security pushed through the crowd toward them, he finally went to check on Cindy like he should have done five minutes earlier.

Nearly hyperventilating again, I stepped toward Axel to see if he was okay. He hadn't fallen or anything and just had a small cut on his face, but I looked him over anyway. Better safe than sorry. After checking every limb not covered by clothes, my nursing mind concluded that all he'd received from this fight was a purple bruise on his cheek. He'd be fine, thank goodness.

As I pulled a band aid from my purse (future nurse, remember?), he grabbed my hand and glanced at Derek nervously. "Is he okay?" he whispered, subtly pulling me away. People standing nearby whispered about what happened as we huddled next to each other. "It sounds like those guys weren't even doing anything. Derek just lashed out."

"That can't be," I whispered back, ignoring his wince as I placed the bandage. "I'm sure he was just protecting her. They may have tried to...I don't know, hurt her or something."

Axel looked unsure but didn't speak again as two police officers arrived to make sure everyone was okay. Derek wasn't charged but he did receive a warning, and I could tell Axel wouldn't forget that punch anytime soon. Our perception of Derek, which had already been negative, was now completely in the red. He'd taken things too far.

I'd have to ask Cindy exactly what happened afterwards. Something didn't sit right with me about this fight. Maybe the author was a teenager who didn't realize how creepy a violent boyfriend could be but that wasn't an excuse for this. I wasn't going to tolerate a personality like that.

Cindy might be wearing rose-colored glasses when it came to Derek, but I wasn't, so if there was the slightest chance he might bring harm to her, I was going to intervene. I didn't care about being "overbearing and clingy" anymore.

Chapter 24

Luckily, nothing else happened over the coming weeks to make Derek lash out again. There were no more fists thrown or curses shouted.

So, to make this feel logical in my mind, I convinced myself Derek saw those men trying to hurt Cindy and lost his cool. That was it, plain and simple. I'd seen such things happen to perfectly normal characters who weren't prone to violence. Plus, even if that situation *did* feel out of the ordinary, it was common in books for the male to get overprotective in ways that didn't happen in real life.

...But this was still real life for *me*. I couldn't make excuses for inappropriate actions just because we were inside a book. After all, there was still a small chance that we weren't in one after all.

So I remained conflicted, trying to find Derek's good points for Cindy's sake, while also warring with the part imagining him turning that fury onto Cindy instead of a mere stranger who ended up in the wrong place at the wrong time.

Thankfully, for my sanity, I clearly wasn't the only one going through this internal dilemma. I noticed that when Axel hung out with us during study breaks or lunch hours, he kept a wary eye on Derek. He was subtle about it so Derek wouldn't notice, but I did, and I found myself relieved that we were on the same page.

The difference Derek's presence made in our group became increasingly apparent in the weeks that followed. He kept everyone, excluding Cindy, on edge. I winced when someone accidentally bumped into us or one of us made a comment Derek may not have liked. What types of things triggered him? Would it happen again?

When midterms approached, I spent all my free time in my dorm or the library with Cindy, studying my butt off and staying away from Derek. Even if having a high grade wasn't required for passing, I still liked getting the best grades I could. It felt satisfying. Plus, it made for a good excuse to self-isolate.

Derek didn't join us for those more intensive study hours. He said it distracted him from his own work, which was fine by me. However, Axel didn't seem to suffer from the same problem. He stuck by me during all my study sessions and even helped with the subjects he was experienced in. He sometimes had a habit of talking while I was trying to read but other than that, I appreciated his presence. It made the contrast between his aura and Derek's unpleasant one all the more obvious.

I didn't mention Derek's outburst at the carnival to Cindy for a few weeks, wanting her to bring it up first, but eventually, I reached a point where I could no longer wait. I had to know what happened and what she thought about it.

It happened on the last day of reading week. I was in the library and had just finished rereading my study sheets, deciding this was a good place to stop. I was confident I'd at least get above eighty percent in all my classes, so after days upon days of constant drilling and memorization, I closed my books and focused on Cindy, who was sitting across the library booth from me. Axel was next to me, watching a video about aliens on his phone, so he didn't look up when I leaned over the table we shared. I only vaguely acknowledged that this leaning thing was something I'd picked up from Axel.

"Cindy," I said, glancing around the rest of the library to make sure Derek wasn't around. We'd managed to snag a corner table on the eighth level—Axel saved it for us earlier—so the chances of Derek finding us on this quieter floor seemed unlikely. This was one of the rare moments when I could be alone with Cindy without the threat of exams hanging over our heads. I could finally ask her about the carnival.

"Cindy, I want to talk about your boyfriend," I said quietly, making Axel pull out his earphones to listen.

Cindy froze. "What about him?" she asked.

"I wanted to talk about what happened a few weeks ago...when we went to the festival." I waited for her to speak, since she was clearly uncomfortable.

"I'm sorry Derek hit Axel," Cindy whispered like it was her fault.

"It's okay—" Axel said, but I cut him off.

"This isn't about that. I need to know what happened to piss him off." I glanced at Axel. "Sorry for interrupting."

He replied with a lopsided grin, "Thank you for apologizing."

I squinted at him. Weirdo.

Anyway, back to Cindy. "So, what happened before we got there? What was it that got him so riled up?"

"Well, I went to a food stand while Derek was in the bathroom, then I got lost on my way back, so I started asking the people around me for directions." Cindy kept staring at the table, avoiding my eyes. Her voice was so quiet I had to strain to hear. "Derek saw those guys talking to me and thought I was in danger, so he lashed out."

That concerned me…a lot. It clearly had Axel worried too. He was listening intently.

"Has he ever acted violently before?" he asked. "To you or anyone else?"

She tilted her head, staring up at the ceiling as she tried to recall. Why was she taking so long to think about it? It should be a no brainer. Abuse wasn't easy to forget unless it was common, right?

I could feel my hands sweating under the table.

"He's never hurt me or anything," Cindy began slowly, pulling a strand of hair behind her ears. "There was one other time he shoved a guy out of the way when we were in the hall."

"Why?" I asked.

"He said the guy was eyeing me up."

"So he shoved him?" Axel chuckled, though it was a dark, nervous one. "That's a little worrying, Cindy."

"I agree." I bit my lip. I didn't want to tell her to dump her boyfriend because of two small incidents but…what if this was a sign of future abuse? What if Cindy did something to piss Derek off next? I could already visualize her cowering in a corner while her boyfriend punched the wall.

I was tempted to think Derek's attitude was just a sign of how the author viewed men, since I'd seen a few movies where the male lead was overprotective to the point where it was concerning, but it would be in poor taste to bring that up now.

"Just be careful," I said, wiping my sweaty hands off on my jeans before reaching across the table and squeezing Cindy's hands. "If he does something like that again, or worse, hits *you* instead, please tell me."

Cindy nodded, though she didn't look sure about my words…or maybe about me. Was Derek turning her against me, talking bad about me behind my back? I didn't want to assume but…

I glanced at Axel, glad he was with us. I might need him to help out if Derek chose to raise a hand to me instead of some random guy in the street. Axel wasn't a fighter, but I hoped his height would at least discourage Derek a little…then again, it hadn't stopped him last time.

I felt wrinkles forming on my brow as I tried to think of a quick and easy solution to this problem. Breaking the two up might make Derek freak out, plus it could be a false alarm. But doing nothing couldn't be the right answer.

Man, I hated being the helpful best friend sometimes. I was supposed to always have a solution in mind. Why did real life have to be so difficult?

Chapter 25

R ight after midterms ended, there came an opportunity for Derek to prove that his violent outburst at the festival had been a one-time thing. I was still on edge around him, as was everyone else, but I was more than happy to be proven wrong. He was supposed to be Cindy's other half, after all—her destined partner. It wasn't possible for her chosen one to be violent.

I was sitting outside the cafeteria with Cindy, finally taking a breather after a week of studying straight, when that moment came. I had just finished my final exam for the second quarter and the others had agreed to meet with me and chill for a bit. The group consisted of Derek, Axel, one of my study buddies, and one of Axel's friends who had gone to the carnival with us.

Axel was lying on the grass next to me. He'd spent the last five minutes whining about how tired he was, though his clear motive was to convince me to let him use my lap as a pillow. I knew this close proximity was just a means to mess with me, as usual, so I made a big deal of ignoring him. That didn't stop him from whining, of course, since he was persistent, but I could be too.

Other than Axel, the rest of us were discussing the exams—how we thought we did and what we planned to do with our free weekend. My secret plans were to sleep in and watch movies in my dorm alone, since Cindy would spend that weekend with Derek's family.

However, midway through that conversation, Axel mentioned a party that would be happening soon, offering a not-so-tempting alternative to my relaxing plans.

"It's tonight," he said to all of us. "It's an end of midterms party, though I think half the people there didn't even show up for the exams."

"Did *you*?" Axel's friend asked him jokingly. Axel proceeded to throw his jacket at him.

"Just because I'm a *joker* doesn't mean I'm—" He paused for dramatic effect to keep us in suspense, "—a *joke* in the classroom," he finished. There were eye rolls all around.

"So, who's going?" he asked, looking very pointedly at me.

I wasn't much of a partier, so I opened my mouth to reject him as I always did, but Cindy answered first.

"I'd like to go," she said. "Best to do it now when we're first-years. We won't have time to experience it later. I've heard having fun gets much harder the further into our majors we go."

I noticed Derek straighten slightly. He did not look pleased about the party. Axel did though.

"Great. I guess that means Derek's coming too, then, and Zilla." He turned his eyes to me and I was pressured to say yes. If Cindy was going, so was I, and Axel knew it.

As the conversation eventually drifted onto other topics and we all eventually went our separate ways, Axel trailed after me as I headed down the path toward my dorm.

"Hey—so—I'm a little worried about Derek," he whispered as we continued down the sidewalk together, passing a few students who didn't pay us any mind. "Do you think he's going to start throwing punches at the party?"

"If you were worried about that, why did you invite him?"

"I didn't invite him. I was inviting you. I just made it a general invitation because I knew you'd say no if I asked directly."

My jaw dropped—to be dramatic, of course, not seriously—and I gave him a look to show him I was not impressed. Then I became serious, because we were both actually worried about the same thing. "I'll try to keep an eye on him," I whispered. "But I'm a little scared too. He didn't hesitate when he hit you so—"

"I'll stay by your side to make sure he doesn't touch you," Axel interrupted, his voice low and gravelly. For once, he wasn't joking around. "I will not let him hurt you and if he tries to, my buddies and I will kick him out."

"I'm more worried about Cindy," I whispered. "Do you think he's...cruel to her in private? I know she said he wasn't but maybe he's threatening her to keep quiet about it."

"That's not the vibe I'm getting. Not yet, at least. I think he was genuinely trying to protect her back then but..." He paused, thinking it over while staring at the blue sky. "Like you said, that could change."

"He wouldn't do that, though," I muttered. "Main characters don't do that. He's just protective. That's all it is. It has to be."

Axel looked down on me, frowning, and shook his head. "This is real life, Zilla. I don't mind your book theory on good days, but this is a serious situation. We need to speak rationally."

"I know." I really did, but I'd stuck with this idea for so long that it felt totally real by this point. I just needed to find the right angle and it would help me prevent dangerous situations. If I figured out how the author worked, I could prevent Cindy from getting into trouble. "I know," I repeated. "Really. I'll see you tonight, Axel."

"Looking forward to it." He waved as I walked off and didn't stop until I'd turned a corner, but there was no smile on his face as he did it.

I hoped nothing would happen tonight. If it did, I wasn't sure what I'd do. I couldn't predict any of this. Derek had leapt completely out of the box I'd placed him in, and I didn't know how to shove him back in.

Chapter 26

I first met up with Derek and Cindy in our dorm before heading over to the party. I wanted to make sure they were actually cool with attending. Derek didn't seem annoyed or anything, so it allowed my panic to subside slightly. He looked like he normally did—a little clumsy, a little out of his element, a little sweet. That teeth-grinding, fist-clenching boy from the carnival was long gone. Hopefully he'd stay gone.

Besides, Cindy looked thrilled about experiencing her first party, so that made me a little more positive about the whole thing. I felt like a chaperone, even though it wasn't my party. The fact that Axel invited us made me feel like I had to ensure things went well, like I was defending Axel's right to stay in our friend group. We shared a strange dynamic now and I wasn't sure I liked it. But I wasn't just coming along to enjoy the party. I was going to guard my best friend from her boyfriend's potential temperament issues.

The party took place in one of the dorms, where two boys had combined their rooms to form one massive space. It was large enough to fit at least fifty students plus enough alcohol to keep them tipsy.

As I stepped through the doorway, dodging a few people who had already started drinking, it became clear that this dorm building belonged to the wealthier kids whose parents could afford to rent the big, fancy spaces. Each room was three times the size of my own. It felt more like a classroom than a bedroom.

It was intimidating to go inside. Everything stank with the bitter scent of alcohol and a little cigarette smoke. There were a lot of bodies in there, filling the place with sticky, humid, sweat-filled air. The darkness certainly didn't help either. There were only a few bright, multicolored lights lining the ceiling and floors. The combination of people, smells, and lighting made the whole place intensely claustrophobic. I only felt slightly better when we managed to push through the crowd to the inside, where things weren't quite as packed.

It wasn't hard to find Axel. Not only was he even taller now, since he'd had a second growth spurt this semester, but he and his group were very loud. Their laughs overpowered the blasting music, which was a feat in itself.

To my surprise, Axel wasn't flirting with a bunch of girls like I'd expected him to. He was instead standing with a few male friends, entertaining them with some hilarious story about goat cheese while he occasionally drank from a black cup. I recognized one of his buddies as the freckled one who came to the carnival. He must not have ended up dating my friend after all, since I hadn't seen them together since.

Axel looked great. His hair was a little messy and his cheeks were pink from drinking but other than that, he stood out from the rest. It was hard to believe he looked even better than he had in high school. The maturity of being a university student suited him… or maybe it was just my proximity to him that gave me that silly idea.

When he turned and spotted me, his eyes lit up. The look of elation on his face made that anxiety spring back into my stomach.

After patting one of his friends on the back, he made a beeline for me, his steps only slightly wobbly. He was definitely tipsy—possibly drunk. Great. My hopes that he'd protect me from Derek just went out the window.

"Hey, Godzilla." He wrapped his arm around my neck casually and nodded at Cindy. I was glad the darkness hid the heat rising up my neck. "I'm so glad you guys came. This party was boring without you."

"Oh?" What an obvious lie. "You looked like you were having fun," I said, pointing at his friends.

Axel groaned and motioned for them to go away even though they were already ten feet back. "Nah. It's not a party 'til you arrive, right?" He flashed his white teeth at me drunkenly, then nodded at Cindy again. "Cindy, can I get you anything? A drink? Where's Derek?"

He was right. Where was Derek? He'd been with us a second ago.

"No thanks, I'm good. Derek went to the bathroom so I'm gonna wait for him over there," she said meekly, pointing at the corner of the room where the single bathroom was. She was acting all shy again. I thought she'd gotten more comfortable around Axel in these last couple of months but something must have changed. Maybe Derek had something to do with it.

"Do you want me to introduce you to some of my friends?" Axel offered, gesturing around the room. He must know a lot of people. As expected, he'd only needed a few months to fill an entire room with new acquaintances.

"No." Cindy started rubbing the upper parts of her arms nervously, glancing around the room but clearly looking for a place to hide rather than people to chat with. "I'm not sure Derek would want me to," she added hesitantly.

"What?" Axel frowned, sobering up. "What's the point of attending a party if you aren't here to meet people?"

I waited for Cindy to answer, wanting to hear it too. *Just admit it's Derek who insists you not talk to people. Confirm it. Please give me a reason to break you two up without feeling like a douche.*

I jumped when a door slammed to our right. I saw Derek exit the bathroom a moment later, wiping his hands on his jeans as he approached. He looked unhappy.

Axel's hand tightened on my shoulder when Derek joined us. Was Axel jealous? Had his crush on Cindy returned? Or was he just nervous Derek might freak out again, like me?

Why had that first thought even popped into my head? Of course he was worried about Derek's freak out! Jealousy wasn't even part of the equation right now. *Get out of my head, dumb writer.*

"Axel. Zilla." Derek nodded at both of us, then pulled Cindy away. "Enjoy the party."

I bristled, wondering if I should recommend we stick together.

"You too!" Axel called drunkenly, then turned back to me once the couple was gone, his grip on me still tight. It felt like I was the one holding him up now. He was still unsteady. "He scares me," he whispered, though his voice was louder than normal. His already loose tongue had somehow gotten looser from the alcohol.

"I think you're overreacting and drunk," I assured him, ignoring how close he was and how his statement mirrored my own thoughts. I had to pretend everything was fine so the situation wouldn't worsen. "Derek hasn't done anything since the carnival so his actions back then must have been a fluke." I hoped. "You smell like alcohol and..." I wrinkled my nose. "Way too much cologne."

"Ah." He laughed, pointing his head at the ceiling. He only did that when he was faking it, so I was surprised he was still doing it while drunk. Interesting. "I wanted to impress you," he slurred, leaning down so we were eye-to-eye. Even in this poor lighting, the blue in his irises shone brightly, making me want to turn away. I only maintained eye contact because I had to remain in control of the situation.

"Well, you failed. Drunk Axel doesn't impress me. You're nearly falling on top of me."

"What if that's part of my plan?" he asked with a giddy smile. Him leaning right on my shoulder reminded me just how much taller he'd gotten since that first night at prom. It also reminded me of what he tried to do to Cindy that night. Now *I* was the one in her position. The only difference was I didn't have a best friend nearby to protect me.

My chest tightened as he continued leaning forward, my heart racing painfully.

We were an inch apart.

Then he closed the gap.

My senses dulled when his lips pressed against mine in a surprisingly gentle kiss. As his arms reached around my back and pulled me closer, I raised my eyebrows and shoved him back with both hands.

"What are you doing? Axel! You're drunk! I am not one of those girls you can just—Nope. I'm not even saying it out loud. You need some water." I turned to look for something non-alcoholic he could drink but he wouldn't let me go. He was much stronger than me, though I could tell even his drunk self had no intention of harming or forcing me.

"I'm sorry, okay? I should have asked first but I knew you'd say no and I—I just wanted to kiss you."

I couldn't help cringing. Thank goodness he didn't act this way when he was sober. "There are plenty of girls here who would be happy to kiss you. Now we need to—"

"But I don't *want* to kiss them. I want to be with *you.*"

"Sober you would not be saying this."

"Of course I wouldn't. I'm a gentleman. But I always *want* to kiss you, even if I don't say it."

This was simultaneously the dumbest conversation I'd ever had and somehow the sweetest too. "Axel, this is embarrassing," I hissed. I tried to put some distance between us, but he kept going, continuing to whine in my ear. He wasn't gripping me too hard, so I could shove him away if I used some force, but that would probably knock him onto his butt. So, instead, I tried pulling him into a corner. At least that way, not *everyone* could see him begging me for a kiss.

I groaned as I pulled this tall, wobbly, whiny man behind me. A few people gave us strange looks, making me relieved none of them attended the gaming club. I would be mortified if one of my friends saw this.

Some party this was turning out to be.

Chapter 27

"Look, I won't remember this tomorrow when I'm sober, so why don't you just fulfil my wish one more time," Axel said, holding up a finger to emphasize the one wish. "Then you can have some dirt on me—Axel Burns is in love with you. It'll make for good blackmail. You love holding things over me, right? Like the book thing and me being a playboy and stuff. This can be just like that."

"I can't hold such an embarrassing thing over your head when it's more embarrassing for *me* than you!" I sighed as he leaned toward me again, placing one hand between me and the wall so I was trapped. So cliché.

I hated this position. It let me see his eyes so clearly and they were filled with a longing I had never seen him aim toward another girl, not even to Cindy in high school.

"I was hoping you wouldn't notice that little detail," he whispered, reminding me of a middle-schooler as he leaned his head against my shoulder, breathing deeply like he felt sick. Maybe he did. "Sorry. I shouldn't be messing with you right now. You can run away if you want to."

"I don't plan to leave you alone, not unless you do something incredibly reprehensible." I sighed, letting him continue to lean on me and praying he wouldn't vomit down my shirt. "Well, since you're being so honest, why don't you get everything else out in the open?" It was kind of cute seeing him lay everything bare. I had always assumed he never hid anything, but apparently not even the most blunt, outgoing person could live without a few secrets. "I know you don't *actually* love me," I began, egging him on, "but there must be some actual secrets you can reveal to me. I can use those as blackmail instead."

To be honest, I wasn't sure if he was lying about the kissing and such. I'd sometimes wondered if he truly was interested in me romantically. He claimed in high school that he never pursued a girl after she rejected him, right? Yet he'd been pursuing me for over a year despite countless pushbacks.

But that could all be an act. Maybe getting me to fall for him was part of a dare or challenge he'd set for himself. That was a typical plotline in books. Granted, it often resulted in the people becoming a couple once they realized they loved each other after all, but this wasn't one of those stories.

"If I unload my secrets upon you, Godzilla, will you let me kiss you?"

"...If it's a good enough secret," I lied, knowing I could still say no after he spilled the beans. I wasn't sure why I was even playing into this, honestly, other than because it was fun to watch him act like a baby.

Also...I...wouldn't hate being kissed by him again.

"Fine. I..." He took a deep breath, about to reveal the greatest secret in existence. "To tell you the truth, Zilla, I—I can't stand bananas."

I snorted, unable to control myself. "That's not nearly good enough. You need to tell me something juicy."

"...I hate boxers."

"Gross but not blackmail material."

"Fine." He leaned away, breaking eye contact so he could take a few more huge breaths. Was he nervous or feeling ready to puke? It could be either. "Fine. I—I don't think you're as mean as you used to be."

That actually made me happy. I thought no one noticed my efforts to be a little nicer to people. "Interesting, but that's not something you're embarrassed about."

"Okay." He looked up at the ceiling, thinking hard and making a grumbling noise like a little boy being forced to apologize. It was terribly adorable.

"Well?" I was actually enjoying with this. It made the head-pounding music and mass of bodies tolerable. Plus, he was between me and the crowd, so I felt a little less trapped.

"I think your theory about the book is really silly," he finally whispered, pressing his forehead against mine. He was burning up.

Maybe he should have kept that one a secret. "Thanks—" I said sarcastically.

"And I think it's adorable," he continued, his words slurring. "And I love hearing you talk about it because you get so worked up...I love it." His voice was lower than a whisper now. "And you."

There was that unfamiliar pang in my chest again, burning me up inside and making me ache to be closer to him. It felt like I'd been cursed by something, some red string that was tugging me toward him despite all my efforts to cut it.

"I love how you're so protective of Cindy even though it doesn't benefit you," he continued, leaning in again and keeping his hands on either side of me. "I love how you tolerated me from the start even though you didn't like me. I love that we've become close friends despite our differences."

"...Thank you, Axel. I could say the same to you." My face was heating up now, and not in a fun way. I no longer felt comfortable in this position. I needed some fresh air...and time to get my feelings back in order.

"And I know you like to think you're not the main character in this life because it takes the pressure off you." He kept going. "I know you'd rather focus on Cindy instead of yourself so you don't have to worry about falling in love or putting yourself out there because you're afraid of getting hurt." Well, that was a little hurtful. "But I—"

"Axel—" I warned, but he wasn't listening. He looked half-asleep now. That or he was just relieved to get this off his chest.

"Every time you talk about Cindy and how she's the most important person in this world, I become so desperate to tell you you're wrong. Well, you're not wrong—Cindy is very nice, but you're important too, Zilla."

I stayed silent because I actually wanted to listen to this. I'd been needing to hear it for a long time.

"And I also want to tell you..." He closed his eyes, leaning forward again.

We were close enough to kiss a second time.

"You've always been the main character to me, Godzilla."

There was a long silence between us, filled with rap music and the pounding of boots on the hardwood floor. I slowed my breathing, trying to come to terms with the fact that after all his talking and whining, instead of pissing me off or pushing me away, he had finally managed to say the right thing. He'd uttered the exact words that broke down my walls and made me fall for him. Despite all my internal protests and reasoning, all my resistance against the author, I had wanted to like him for a long time. I just needed to hear him say the right words and believe he truly meant them.

I wasn't just a side character to him or anyone else. I wasn't a girl in a box whose sole purpose was to stand by while the main character fell in love. My entire existence wasn't reliant on Cindy's.

All this time, Axel had been looking at me instead of Cindy. He viewed me as more than my stereotypical traits. He didn't love me because I was stubborn or easy to tease. He loved me for me.

Dang it! This wasn't how things were supposed to go.

My heart was completely on fire. No one could see it, but I had totally fallen for him and was very upset about it. This was the one man I had promised myself I'd never fall for. He was the last person I ever expected to love.

Axel opened his eyes and peeked at me like a kid and my heart raced. "So, is that secret good enough for a kiss?" he asked cheekily.

"Was it..." I gulped and cleared my throat. "Was it the truth?"

"Of course it was."

"Then..." I raised my chin, holding onto my stubbornness just a little longer. "You'll have to tell me those exact words again when you're sober. Then I'll actually believe it." I believed it now, but he'd worked this hard. He shouldn't mind waiting a little longer.

"I will." He smirked. "But we agreed. One secret equals one kiss to be cashed in right away."

And I really wanted to honor that agreement. "Fine." Hopefully no one around us could see or hear me give in. "You can. Just once."

He smiled, that silly one he only did when we were actually having fun together instead of bickering, and leaned in so I couldn't see his expression anymore. Then he froze right in front of me, heaved, and backed away quickly.

"Don't take this the wrong way but I think I'm gonna be sick," he whispered, instantly sending panic through my chest instead of warmth.

"You have got to be kidding me." After two years of chasing, he had finally managed to catch me and he chose this exact moment to puke?

I kept my anger at bay, since most of it was overshadowed by my swooning anyway, and led him to the bathroom. Once we reached it, with his back convulsing from holding in his dinner, I pushed him inside. He nearly tripped when I did but caught himself just in time so I wouldn't have to catch him. Then I slammed the door behind him and stood guard outside, my arms crossed and mind replaying everything he'd just said to me.

What was I going to do after this? Date him?

I desperately wanted to. I'd wanted to for some time.

But this was Axel Burns we were talking about. I'd seen him make out with seven different girls *while* he was dating someone else.

Well, knowing Axel, we'd discuss this whole topic together once he was sober. I knew he'd bring it up immediately...unless he forgot. What if he was one of those guys who forgot everything when he was drunk? Then *I'd* have to be the one to bring it up. That would be humiliating.

I was sitting there, sweating as I pictured that conversation, when I heard my name called amidst all the other voices and looked up. My eyes widened as I spotted Cindy rushing toward me, looking panicked. Something had just gone terribly wrong, and I was pretty sure that something started with a capital D.

Chapter 28

Cindy was pale and a little shaky, one hand clinging to the hem of her jacket like it was all that was keeping her from falling apart. I immediately pulled her close and away from the crowd as I tried to figure out what happened. I could already venture a guess but had to confirm before I started yelling at Derek.

"What's wrong?" I asked, looking for her boyfriend. "Where's Derek?"

"I need to talk to you," she whispered, leaning close so only I could hear. "Zilla, I—"

"Cindy!"

We both jumped when Derek emerged from the mass of people. He grabbed my best friend's arm and pulled her away from me. "Don't run off like that. We're leaving."

"Leaving?" We'd only been at the party for twenty minutes. "You just got here!" I shouted over the music.

"Yeah, and you can stay here with your drunk boyfriend if you want. Cindy and I are leaving," he said again, nearly spitting at me as he shouted. Why was he so pissed? I hadn't done anything. More importantly, what had Cindy just tried to tell me? "We never should have come," he continued as he led Cindy toward the door.

"Did something happen?" I asked, trying to keep my tone neutral to avoid upsetting him. "I can help—"

"Just stay out of our lives, Zilla! I've told you this before! Leave us alone!"

Cindy's face was totally white as Derek pressed her against his chest. He glared at me, reminding me of that time in the library when he lectured me for sticking too close.

As Derek and I stared each other down, I heard Axel return from the bathroom and come to a stop behind me. His presence at my back instantly calmed me but it only made the situation escalate.

I leaned against him, reassured when he wrapped his arms around me defensively.

"Something wrong, Derek?" Axel asked, his voice deeper than normal. The slur was gone, as was his wobbly footing.

Derek just smirked and wrinkled his nose. "You stink, Axel. I'm not sure I want you around Cindy when you're this drunk. You might try to assault her again."

Axel frowned and pulled me closer. "Are you serious? What is your problem, man?"

Derek shook his head like Axel was the one in the wrong. "This shouldn't even need to be said, but stay away from my girlfriend."

"Derek—" Cindy whispered.

"Both of you need to stay away! All you two do is cause stress for Cindy."

What?

"Let's go." Derek dragged Cindy out of the room and I immediately tried to go after them. I only stopped when Axel tightened his grip on my arm.

"Don't follow him yet," he whispered. "I'm worried he'll hurt you."

"He might hurt *her*! I don't even know why he's so pissed."

"He's jealous and mentally unstable. I don't know. Look, we'll follow them from afar, okay? If it looks like he's gonna hurt you or Cindy, we'll call the police." Axel turned me around so I was facing him and looked into my eyes. "Trust me, okay?"

I wanted to, but Cindy came to *me* for help and I had allowed her to be dragged off. I'd been too scared to do anything and it filled me with shame. That wasn't how a best friend was supposed to act. "We're leaving," I insisted. "Right now!"

"Okay." He didn't resist this time as I shoved my way through the crowd and back into the hallway. When Derek and Cindy were nowhere to be seen, I headed out of the building completely, entering the cold, dark parking lot behind the dorm. They weren't out there either. I'd just missed them.

Now I was full-on panicking with quick breaths, a fuzzy head, and a ringing in my ears. I had to lean against Axel again, needing something stable to prevent my legs from slipping.

"They may have gone to our dorm," I whispered. "Can you come with me?"

"Sure."

"Wait, no. On second thought, you shouldn't come. I don't want him to see you and flip out." Derek might hit him again.

"Nope. We're going together, right now."

I had been hoping he'd say that because even though I wanted to keep Axel safe, I *really* didn't want to go in there alone. I was so glad he was by my side.

Chapter 29

"If she's not there, I'm calling the cops," I whispered as we ran hand-in-hand down the concrete path that would eventually lead us to our dorm. I hoped Cindy was there but if the place was empty, I would take that as a sign that Derek had kidnapped her. Then I'd get the police involved. I wasn't going to wait around and give Derek the benefit of the doubt. He'd had one chance and he squandered it.

Luckily, it didn't have to come to that.

I unlocked the door with my keycard and pushed it open, making sure Axel was behind me before doing so. Then I hurried inside and found Cindy sitting on her bed, cheeks stained red but face white as the sheets beneath her. Derek was nowhere to be seen.

It was a false alarm...for now.

Maybe I'd been wrong about Derek after all...again...hopefully.

"Cindy. Are you okay?" I whispered, pulling Axel in. I locked the door behind us after checking both ends of the hall for her boyfriend. "Is Derek gone?"

"He's gone," she whispered. "He was just mad, that's all. He went home."

"Are you sure?" I asked, nervously peeking out the window. It overlooked the dorm parking lot and while there were plenty of dirt and salt-covered cars down there, I couldn't see any sign of the brown-haired man.

As I took a seat next to Cindy on the bed, Axel pulled Cindy's desk chair up to the door and sat on it like a guard dog. If Derek decided to barge back in, Axel would get to him first.

"What made him mad, Cindy?" I prodded, watching her face for any sign she wasn't being honest. Cindy wasn't the type to tell falsehoods but if someone was pressuring her, especially someone she loved, I was sure she could do it. The only consolation was she wouldn't make a good liar.

Cindy didn't answer, choosing to fiddle with the hair tie around her wrist instead.

"Tell me what happened, Cindy. Please. How long has he been acting like this?"

She hesitated again, rubbing her arms and glancing out the window. "Since the carnival."

"And what's he been doing? Just getting mad or...more?"

"He'll yell a little bit and...he hit a guy again. Just once, when we were at a restaurant. Then I saw him glaring at another guy during the party and thought he might do it again so I—" She gulped, eyes glazing over.

I shook my head in disgust and glanced at Axel, who looked like a deer caught in headlights. He had no clue how to respond to this. Neither did I.

"Has he ever hurt you?" I hissed, angry for her now.

"No! He would never!" Cindy shook her head, blinking rapidly. "He loves me. He's just stressed from school. Now that midterms are over, he'll calm down. I'm sure of it."

"Well, *I'm* not sure of it." I placed my hand over hers, squeezing like I did a few weeks back. "I'm getting really worried about you. Maybe you two should take a break. He might need therapy or—"

"This is just temporary," Cindy insisted, more forcefully this time. "We love each other! He would never hurt me, okay? Stop worrying about me."

She was beginning to sound like Derek.

"Well, maybe you and I should stay at Axel's place for a few nights, just in case he gets mad again and—"

"No! That's stupid, Zilla. If you do that, he really *will* get mad." She shook her head and, for the first time, looked at me like *I* was the dumb, illogical one. "Derek was right, Zilla. Sometimes, you *do* need to mind your own business. I think this is one of those times."

"I'm just worried you might be in danger—"

"I can handle myself, Xiang!" Cindy yanked her hand away and it stung, not because she'd physically hurt me but because this was the first time she'd ever pushed me away. We'd never spoken to each other like this before. We'd been friends our whole lives. Was Derek more important than a lifetime of friendship?

"Can you...sleep somewhere else tonight?" Cindy whispered. "I want to be alone."

I cast a distressed look at Axel, who immediately got up from his guard spot. "She can stay at my place. We have a couch in our dorm and a private shower. It's..." His voice trailed off as I rose too. He knew I didn't want to go but had no choice.

"Okay. I'm...I'm sorry, Cindy," I whispered, not sure what I'd even done wrong but unable to bear getting yelled at again. I could handle plenty of arguments with Axel but not with her. Cindy and I never ended a fight without making up. It was unheard of.

This morning, everything had felt right with the world. Exams had ended, our group had hung out and laughed about our classes, and the boy I liked had professed his love for me. Now, in the confusing span of a few minutes, I'd lost my best friend and might have to abandon her in a vulnerable position.

Axel's love confession from earlier wasn't even present in my mind anymore. The butterflies in my stomach had turned to lead.

I stayed silent as I grabbed a change of clothes and my toothbrush, then Axel led me to his five-person dorm in a separate building across campus. It was only a five-minute walk, but it felt like twenty because I was so afraid of encountering Derek along the way.

Finally, after riding the elevator together in silence, we reached Axel's empty dorm. It was much bigger than mine, though that was probably because he shared the space with several boys rather than just one like I did with Cindy. The shared kitchen and living room we entered, which connected to five bedrooms, was also cleaner than I expected, though now that I thought about it, Axel was always a clean and put together guy. It made sense that his living space looked the same. The more shocking part was that five different men all managed to stay clean. I'd heard nightmare stories about college roommates being slobs.

After a quick discussion, Axel decided he'd sleep on the couch since it was part of the shared living space, which meant any of his roommates could walk past him on their way to the kitchen or bathroom. He said he'd feel more comfortable knowing I was asleep in a room with a lock. So, after brushing my teeth and forgoing a shower, I crawled under his navy-blue covers and stared at the ceiling, my mind racing with a variety of thoughts and none of them good. The pillow and sheets smelled like his cologne. There luckily weren't any bitter alcoholic smells here like there were on his clothes today. The aftermath of the party hadn't followed him into his living space.

As I lay there, staring at his blue ceiling and listening to one of his roommates snore through the wall, I pondered what the cliché best friend in a book would have done if she'd learned what I had. Would she be stubborn and insist on helping the main character, even if her help was unwanted? Or would she back down and let the main character handle things alone?

I couldn't think of one book where this situation happened. If abuse did take place in a book, it was usually brushed off or descended into the plot of a thriller rather than a romance. There was no blueprint for this.

What was I supposed to do? I hated that even after years of studying romance novels, there was no set plotline for me to follow.

The romance books, and the clear lines of dialogue and clichés that came with them, had been the only stable thing in my life. Boy meets girl, boy falls for girl, they date and live happily ever after. So what happened if the boy turned out to be a villain? And what if there was no confirmed evidence to prove it? What if Cindy was right about Derek and I was wrong? What if there was a planned redemption arc that I couldn't foresee?

I hated losing the one line of stability that had been present for years. Now the only thing in my life that made sense was Axel. That was a twist I never expected.

Chapter 30

That following morning was exceedingly awkward. As I sat in the middle of Axel and his roommates' tiny kitchen, hanging off the edge of one of their three plastic chairs beside a stained table, I nibbled on some toast Axel had made for me. Axel's roommates tried to creep around me as they got ready for class. It was clear they weren't sure if I was there because something was wrong or because I was a one-night stand. As rude as it was to do so, I ignored them. I had zero mental energy to spare for politeness.

Once they were gone and I finished my toasted raisin bread with butter, I looked Axel in the eye. He was seated across from me, plate empty. He'd polished off three slices of toast in half the time it took me to finish one. He looked nervous now, like he had just remembered our kiss yesterday and was worried I was about to reject him, but I had other things to focus on. That kiss could wait. Plus, I wasn't even sure how I wanted to respond yet.

"I'm going to check on her," I said, pushing away my plate and rising.

"No." He nearly knocked over his chair trying to stop me. "She needs some time to think this through. And you might…" He paused, studying my face to figure out what I was thinking, then he pointed at my face. "I know that look. You're thinking about the book again, aren't you?"

"...If this was a serial killer book the whole time, or something about abuse, it would—"

"Zilla." He sounded exhausted. "I know this is your method for dealing with stressful things in your life, but let's be serious for a moment. This isn't a game and Cindy isn't some tool in a narrative. You have to wait for her to ask for help. If you interfere, it might drive her further away."

"Derek's manipulating her. I know you can see it. Besides, what if he hits her? Or worse?"

"Then she'll ask you for help."

"It might be too late by then! I'm sorry, Axel. Sometimes you're right and I'm wrong but this is one point where I will never agree to disagree. Abuse victims don't always ask others for help, especially when their abuser alienates them from everyone else. That might be what's happening here. Cindy's the type to think the best of others. She might not fight back against Derek until it's too late. If I'm wrong, great, but if I'm right, she could be in serious trouble." I grabbed the few things I'd brought with me, determined to see this through. "I'm not going to wait around for something to happen, Axel. I'd hate myself if I found out she died when I could have done something to prevent it." Maybe I was overreacting. I hoped I was. That would be better than being right. But I couldn't be sure I was.

I reached for the door when Axel stepped in front of me.

"...Zilla...If you're doing this, we should call the police first—"

"I just need to talk to her and convince her to leave him. Getting the police involved will make her life so much harder." I didn't have time to argue anymore. Every second wasted here could mean an extra punch or mile.

"I'm calling the police regardless," Axel insisted, not taking his hand off the door, continuing to block my way. "I'm not letting you go in there alone and as much as I'd like to protect you, I don't think I can if Derek is as violent as we think he is."

I really didn't want it to come to that. "Axel—"

"You need to value your life, Zilla."

"And you need to value Cindy's." Cindy was and always should be the priority, not just because she was the focus of this story but because she was one of the few people in this world that I cared about.

Axel's jaw jutted out slightly. He was grinding his teeth, frustrated. "Either you let me call the police or I'm not letting you leave this room."

We stood there, staring each other down, until I finally relented. It would be better to have too much protection than none at all. Plus, I understood Axel's concern. I always got annoyed in the movie theater when characters chose to hunt down the killer alone rather than call the cops. Derek wasn't a serial killer, though. He was just a guy with a temper. The worst he could do was hit me and I could take it. Cindy couldn't, though.

"Fine," I conceded quietly. "We can call the police, but only if she's not in her room."

"Obviously." Axel relaxed, then grabbed his wallet and phone from the table. Now that we'd both calmed down, we could stop overreacting. "You should call her first."

"Agreed."

I did so, dialing her number from muscle memory. It was the only number I had memorized other than my mom's.

It rang three times. Four. Five. She normally didn't wait that long to pick up.

Finally, she answered.

"Zilla?" Her voice sounded strained, like she'd been crying.

"Hey," I began nervously. "I'm sorry about yesterday—"

"Zilla," she croaked, barely above a whisper. "Something's wrong."

I froze and looked up at Axel, eyes wide. "Cindy, what's wrong?" I asked, trying to keep my voice low but also letting Axel know what was happening... "Is—"

Then I heard it—another voice a few feet away from her. It sounded like Derek.

"Who are you talking to?" I faintly heard him ask.

"Just Zilla—"

Derek said something I couldn't discern, his voice lined with agitation, then Cindy hung up.

"Derek's with her," I said immediately, locking my phone and grabbing Axel's arm. "He made her hang up."

"Okay." Axel nodded. "Then it's time to actually do something about this. Did she say where she was?"

I shook my head, blood rushing to my ears. "I didn't get a chance to ask."

"Then we'll check your dorm and his. Which one do you want to go to first?" He spoke while dialing the number for campus security on his phone.

"Should we split up?" I asked, though it sounded stupid as soon as it exited my mouth. Splitting up was always the dumbest move, even though we could cover more ground that way.

Axel shook his head, mercifully not giving me a judgmental look as he started speaking to whoever answered on the other end of the line. While he did that, letting security know the situation and where Cindy might be, I tried to slow my breathing and regain control of my thoughts.

Okay. I'd been right all along. Cindy was in danger. Derek's true colors must have finally surfaced and now that the cat was out of the bag, he wasn't going to let Cindy leave him. Maybe his jealousy was the cause of these outbursts, or his overprotectiveness. The author's character must have gotten away from her, forming a mind of his own and growing out of control—

No. I shouldn't think about the book or author right now. It wasn't helping the situation. Maybe it never had.

"Let's go to my dorm first," I said once Axel hung up. "I'll grab my pepper spray if she's not there. He's just one guy, right? Two against one."

"Three against one," Axel said, opening the door to lead us out. "Don't underestimate Cindy."

I couldn't help smiling at him. He was starting to sound like me.

"We need to hurry."

Chapter 31

When I arrived at my dorm to procure some self-defense sprays my father had insisted I bring to university, I peeked into our room. Just as I feared, Cindy was gone, as was her phone and some of her clothes judging by how empty the closet looked.

"He took her," I said to a very concerned Axel, who was waiting outside the door. "We should check his dorm first, but if he's not there—"

"We'll find her," he assured me without hesitation before holding my hand. "Is there anything else you need?"

"No." I shook my head, blood pounding loud enough in my ears to nearly block out his voice.

As we rushed down the hall, we passed a tall security guard, who was clearly headed toward my and Cindy's room. Axel paused to explain to the man that the room was empty and we planned to head to Derek's dorm, but as soon as Axel mentioned where he and I were headed, the burly man raised a hand to stop us.

"I'll let my partner know where to look. She's already on her way there. You two should stay here, where it's safe."

No. I couldn't leave Cindy alone. She had called *me* first, not security or 911 (which was a bit foolish on her part but showed who she trusted most). "Can we at least come with you?" I asked, trying and failing to banish the shakiness in my voice.

The man frowned, looking both sympathetic and unwilling to budge. "The most I can do is let you stand outside the building, but if he's armed, you'll still be in danger. I suggest you head to the security station. It's a five-minute walk from here—right beside the cafeteria. If we find your friend, we'll bring her there."

"And what if you don't find her?" I whispered, more to myself than him. I didn't know any hangouts or hideouts Derek frequented. He and I were never real friends. We didn't discuss those kinds of things. Plus, I only met Cindy in our dorm and the library. I didn't know where she went with Derek when I wasn't around.

"We'll keep looking and get the police involved if we can't find him," the man assured me. I saw him softening so he said one more thing. "I'm asking you to stay in a safe location so you don't get hurt. It's much easier to search for *one* person than three."

I knew he was right and I should do what he said. I was supposed to be the logical one here. Acting irrational or frightened was Cindy's role, right? Yet here I was, ready to charge into danger. After all, what was the worst Derek could do to me? Punch me? I didn't fear a bruise or two.

"We'll go," Axel said, placing his arm across my back to keep me steady and signify that he'd lead me to safety. "We don't want to hold you up further."

"Right." The security guard nodded, scrutinized us one more time, then headed back the way he'd come. Only after he was gone did Axel lower his hand.

"We can wait outside the dorm in case he tries to escape," Axel whispered.

"We're not going to the security building?"

Axel shook his head. "Nah. I don't want to sit around either now that we've got the ball rolling."

That was a little surprising. He was finally living up to the rebellious stereotypes I'd given him when we first met.

"I don't plan to put us in any danger," Axel added, "but I don't want to risk letting him get away either. Plus, I owe him a punch, right?" He smirked at me, clearly trying to lighten the mood. Luckily, I was eager for comfort and help.

So we headed downstairs and out the back door, toward Derek's dorm. I made us circle around the campus on the way so we'd end up passing his car. If he had already taken it, we could warn security. I hadn't thought to tell the guards about it, but it was too late now. We were almost there. If Derek planned to make a getaway, we'd be there to stop him.

This was a horrible idea.

I should have brought a taser.

Chapter 32

J ust as I feared, I heard a commotion as we neared the lot where Derek's car was parked. It was a red sedan that he'd purchased specifically for the years he planned to spend in Canada with Cindy. As we approached the parked car, I spotted two figures rushing toward it from the other end of the lot.

The sky was full of dark clouds and the scent of rain hung in the air, so it was too dark to see the couple's faces clearly, but I'd known Cindy for most of my life. I could recognize her gait in a second. Her small and hesitant steps contrasted Derek's long, angry strides.

"It's them," Axel said, quickening his pace as I pulled my pepper spray from my purse. "Stay back, Zilla. Give me the spray."

I hesitated. My dad had made me practice. Did Axel even know how to use it properly? It might be better to do it myself. My dad forced me to practice before I moved.

Axel's stance told me he had asked for the spray because he didn't want to see me in danger, but I felt the same way about him.

The moment of hesitation hurt us, and by the time I handed him the can, I could hear the beep of the Derek unlocking the car. We were still a good fifty feet away, hidden from Derek's sight behind other vehicles. We wouldn't have time to stop him if we didn't act right now.

"I don't like this," Cindy was whimpering as I heard a car door open. I sprinted toward the sound, scanning the ground for a rock or stick to use as a weapon. Sadly, there was nothing. I only had Axel and my fists to protect Cindy.

"We'll be fine," Derek insisted before slamming the car door, presumably locking Cindy in. His words were identical to Axel's earlier ones, but while Axel's had been lined with worry and a need to comfort, Derek's were harsh and panicked. I began to wonder if he loved Cindy at all. If the author's goal was to make Derek fulfil the role of a loving boyfriend, this was the most messed up and twisted way it could be carried out. Derek's words sounded stilted, odd. He was treating her like a dog protecting a bone, rather than a man protecting a woman.

"I don't want to go," Cindy insisted, her voice muffled by the car.

Outraged, I swerved around a car, still behind Axel, and finally got a good view of the situation. Derek was circling around the vehicle to the driver's side so he could get in and take Cindy away. He might be planning to take her all the way to the States or to some hotel far enough away that I couldn't find her. I had no idea. There were no clues as to what his endgame was.

I considered shouting at Derek to stop, hoping it would delay him, but that would give away Axel's element of surprise, so I kept my voice and footsteps quiet as I continued weaving between cars.

As soon as Derek touched the handle of the driver's door, Axel reached him. He grabbed his shoulder and yanked Derek back, away from the vehicle. Derek grunted in surprise, raising his hands defensively, but before he could cover his face, Axel raised the spray can.

Derek's reaction time was faster than Axel's, which didn't surprise me all that much. As soon as Derek spotted the pepper spray, he changed his defensive tactics and landed a punch on Axel's shoulder at the same moment Axel pressed down on the can. The liquid shot out and hit Derek in the eyes, making him scream and wave his fists around like a wild animal.

"Cindy!" I shouted as Derek blindly punched Axel again, this time in the chest. Axel fell to his knees, gasping.

"Cindy, get out of the car!" I reached for the spray can Axel had dropped during the scuffle, but Derek kicked it away, then aimed his foot in my direction and landed a solid kick in my torso. I stumbled into Axel.

I heard Cindy scream in genuine terror but by the time I had righted myself and looked up, Derek had yanked the car door open and was sitting in the driver's seat. He glared at me, red faced and panting from the adrenaline, before slamming the car door. I saw him shout something at Cindy—probably telling her to shut up and stay still—but he turned on the engine at the same time so I couldn't hear him. I had to stand there dumbly while Derek reversed out of the parking spot. Cindy was trying to get the car door open from her side, but Derek must have used a child safety lock to keep her trapped.

"Cindy!" I threw the pepper spray can at the car but it bounced off the side window, useless. The car then sped out of the driveway before I could even think about running after it. What could I do against a car anyway? Jump in front of it and break my legs? I didn't think Derek was above running me over at this point.

"I'm sorry," Axel whispered as he rose, one hand pressed to his stomach. The other was pulling his phone out of the pocket of his jeans.

"We have to go after her," I insisted. "Do you have a car?"

He hesitated, then glanced at the other vehicles. "A rental," he said slowly. "But car chases are beyond dangerous, Zilla, and I doubt we can catch up to him anyway. I'm calling the cops this time."

"No." I pressed both hands to my eyes, feeling tears start to leak out. "We can't just call the police."

I wasn't thinking logically, I knew, but there was a reason I was speaking in such an irrational way. I knew the author wouldn't be satisfied if we just called the cops and waited here. Readers didn't like seeing unrelated people complete the rescue. It had to be me. If there wasn't sufficient drama in the story, the author would do something worse later on to force me into a corner. She might put Cindy in even more danger because I chose the easy, intelligent route.

"Why not?" Axel asked, looking at me like I was crazy. "Do you know something I don't?"

I stopped to stare at him, my cheeks streaked with fresh tears. He wouldn't understand. He wouldn't believe me. We both knew where the other stood on this topic. "It's the—she—"

His face dropped, overcome with unfortunate understanding. "Zilla, this is real life. I need you to focus on Cindy right now and what's best for her!"

"I...I know." He was right. We'd been through this before.

I couldn't allow the author to turn me into some mindless, out-of-character cliché. I wasn't dumb enough to avoid the cops. Besides, there was a chance, however small, that there *was* no author pulling the strings. I couldn't be reckless on the off chance that she might sabotage things further.

That was what I told myself as Axel waited, 911 already dialed into his phone. He was waiting for my permission call.

I gulped.

We weren't in a book. There was no evil teenage author pulling the strings. Calling the police would protect Cindy. I forced myself to acknowledge that this whole book farce was just a fantasy I made up in my head, an excuse to explain away weird coincidences. It was time to grow up and move on for good, for Cindy's sake.

"Call them," I said, feeling my throat close up as soon as the words left my mouth. Tears stung my eyes. I had either saved Cindy's life or destroyed it. I hated that my brain was leaning toward the latter.

Axel hit CALL and removed his other hand from his stomach so he could pull me into a sideways hug. For a second, I had been afraid he'd hate me for bringing up the book theory in such a perilous situation, but he chose to squeeze me against him instead, not saying anything as I started to sob.

I allowed myself to cry, unleashing years of anxiety into his shoulder as he gave information to the officers. Then, when his other arm was free, he wrapped it around me too. It was exactly what I needed.

I prayed for Cindy's safety as we exited the parking lot together. If the author killed her because of my actions, I would personally crawl through the pages and strangle her.

Chapter 33

We did end up going to the security building after all, or rather, Axel led me and I spent the entire time shivering with my teeth chattering. It wasn't cold but my body was reacting as though it was. This was the first time I had gone into shock or whatever this panicked feeling was. My heart wouldn't stop racing, even after sitting on a wooden bench inside the security office lobby, which consisted of a tiny room connected to another by a glass screen. There was a woman on the other side, dressed in a black uniform with the university's name on her chest, but after Axel explained the situation, she didn't pay us any mind other than offering some water.

My mind kept picturing every horrible way Cindy could die. Derek could accidentally, or intentionally, crash the car while fleeing the police. Cindy might get the door open and leap out, only to get killed when she hit the road because the car was going too fast. Derek could lock her up in some house where no one would ever find her and she'd die alone in a cold, dark room. The possibilities were endless and my imagination was far too talented.

Axel kept my hand clasped in his the entire time. His fingers felt warm against my freezing ones. He didn't say a word as we leaned against each other, which I was grateful for.

By the time an hour passed and there was no news, I started begging the nameless author, in my head, to let Cindy live. When that didn't work and I came to detest the author more and more, I started praying to God instead. It was what Cindy would have done.

She didn't deserve this. Being naïve wasn't a crime that deserved death.

On the third prayer muttered under my breath, a new security guard finally entered through the front door and approached us. She was a tall woman dressed in navy blue and wearing a calm, empty smile on her otherwise expressionless face. I jumped when she tapped my shoulder.

"We've received news," she said, then annoyingly paused instead of finishing right away. "They found Cindy Annabelle."

My grip on Axel tightened. Dead or alive?

"Derek Daniels has been arrested and she's on her way here. We've contacted her parents. Is there anyone else you think we should call?"

I was so overcome with relief that I just shook my head and leaned against Axel, feeling ridiculously tired despite it being early afternoon. She was okay. Derek had been arrested. We'd never have to worry about him again.

My eyelids were drooping when Cindy herself entered the building twenty minutes later. Her hair was frazzled and her face was white but she smiled as soon as she saw me, which I took as an invitation to rush forward and hug her. She didn't start crying until I squeezed her tight, all the images of her corpse on a road finally fading.

"I'm sorry for pushing you away," she whispered. "I'm so sorry. You were right. I was just scared of losing you both. I didn't want to choose between you and Derek."

"It's okay." It would *all* be okay.

As she sobbed into my shoulder, I peered over her head at Axel, who was grinning at our reunion like a proud parent. He winked at me, probably thinking something like "Thank goodness neither of us will have to put up with Derek's annoying personality anymore" or some other cheeky line that was intended to make my eyes roll.

He was right to smile, though.

This would mark the beginning of a new chapter in Cindy's life…and mine. Derek wasn't her fated person after all, which meant we weren't in a book as I'd assumed for years. That meant the next time she got a boyfriend, I wouldn't feel the need to brush away red flags just because their meeting felt like a picture-perfect storybook. There would be no more excuses made because of co-incidences.

And that change went for me too. I wouldn't push Axel away just because he and I made the perfect side character love story come to life. Axel didn't care about any of that, so I shouldn't either.

PART THREE

Chapter 34

In the next month or two, I went from seeing Cindy a couple times a week to every single day. She had, in her own words, become so used to spending time with Derek that she didn't know what to do with herself now that he was gone, so I started spending every waking hour with her. We studied together, cooked meals together in our shared microwave and toaster, and went out to coffee at least three times a week. We'd sometimes chat late into the night before I turned off the lights and tried to go to sleep.

Those nights were the hardest, as Cindy would sometimes wake up screaming because she was back in that car with Derek, though in those dreams, Derek would reach his destination and the police would never come. The location always changed, ranging from dark apartments and cabins to literal graves. I had to be the one to comfort her every time and after a while, I considered contacting a therapist. I called her parents once to update them on the situation, but they thought that, at least right now, returning to normalcy might be the best thing for Cindy. Plus, going back to our home-town might mean running into Derek again, or at least his family. That would definitely make things worse. It was safer here, several states and an international border away from her now ex.

After that whole kidnapping fiasco was cleared up, I eventually began asking Cindy questions to figure out how their relationship had spiraled so quickly. I discovered, after a little time and prodding, that Cindy and Derek's relationship had been great at first, just like the picture-perfect love story in romance novels, but the move to university was when things went downhill. The changes and stress of schooling brought out the worst in Derek, and coupled with his jealousy towards Axel and annoyance towards me, he started isolating her from everyone she cared about. This came in the form of criticizing me and convincing Cindy I hated having her around. This wasn't true, of course, but since I was the only friend she had besides Derek, Cindy had no one else to turn to and ask advice from, so there wasn't much she could say to defend me.

That was the first step. Derek didn't start getting violent until the carnival, though. After that event set him off, he started hitting other men they encountered in the street or at school, just like Cindy had told us previously. She revealed that Derek occasionally would threaten *her* too, though he always relented at the last second. Cindy told me Derek only lashed out a couple times, but it had been more common than she initially let on. The reason she never told me was because she didn't want to put me in danger.

After Cindy told me how far Derek took things, I commented that he would have turned his fist toward her at some point if things carried on that way. I was hoping to reassure her that leaving him had been the right decision, since I knew she still missed him, but I shouldn't have said it so soon. Rather than comfort her, it made her burst into tears.

"I loved him," she told me as I rubbed her back and held her while she sobbed on my bed. "I still do sometimes."

"I know," I said, even though I couldn't truly understand. She and I were completely different people. We reacted to things differently. While I couldn't see myself ever ending up in her position, I didn't blame her for falling into the trap. Not even I had seen all the warning signs; not until it was too late, at least. So I didn't criticize her when she admitted she still loved him. All I could do was stay by her side and hope things got better over time.

She'd meet some better man someday and he could show her what she was missing.

That might not be for a while, though. So for now, *I* would have to comfort her.

Axel was there to help too, of course, but he didn't have the connection Cindy and I did. He still sat with us for lunch or study breaks sometimes, but I didn't see him around nearly as much now that the chaos was over.

I wasn't sure if it hurt his feelings that he wasn't a priority now that my best friend had returned, but I hoped he understood my dilemma and knew that this would, hopefully, be temporary. Cindy would heal one day and then I could confront Axel about our relationship, but until then, I needed to be there whenever Cindy needed me.

Unfortunately, I was so busy with school and Cindy that I didn't get to talk to Axel about our temporary separation until a month had passed. It did nag at me that he'd confessed his feelings during that party and I never responded, but that wasn't really my fault. Derek was totally the criminal here...even though I had kind of used the disaster as an excuse to avoid giving him an answer. However, I could only run away from Axel for so long. Eventually, he confronted me about what happened between us and where it would lead.

It happened four weeks after the incident. He and I were walking away from the gaming club after a fun two hours of board games and Mario Kart. My phone was in my pocket, out of sight, and Axel was kicking a stone down the path, casual as ever.

"You should invite Cindy to join us next week," he told me, missing the pebble with his foot and taking a step back so he could kick it again. "I think it would do her some good to meet a few new people."

I turned to squint at him, not sure if he was turning into Derek by trying to split us apart. Was he tired of me hanging out with Cindy all the time?

No. That was just me being paranoid after what Derek did. Of course more friends would be good for Cindy, just as they were for me. It was a shame I no longer believed the author was real, because it would have made a good excuse for why I was having such a horrible thought about Axel.

Sadly, Axel read my sassy expression perfectly and immediately chuckled before I could get rid of the furrowed brow and pout.

"Don't be like that. I'm not trying to have you all to myself by forcing her to make friends. I just think it would be good for her to get to know some other girls. It's not healthy for people to be alone, especially when they're still recovering."

"I agree and I've invited her before." I was relieved he had good intentions behind his words, unlike Derek. The déjà vu still lingered, though. "But she's not ready."

"What do you think's holding her back?" Axel asked softly. "Is there anything I can do to help?"

"I…" I bit my lip, completely at a loss. I wanted to help her too. I really did. She had cried again last night. It wasn't even from nightmares. She was just crying over Derek. "I don't know what to do, Axel. I tried to convince her to go to therapy but she doesn't want to, and—" I felt a sob creeping up my throat and shut my mouth to trap it in. I'd heard enough crying for one month. I didn't want to add to it.

"It'll be okay." Axel pulled me into a gentle, cautious hug. He rested his chin on my head as he waited for me to calm down. "Maybe there *is* something I can do to help," he said after my breathing slowed.

"What?"

"My friend is coming over to visit," he explained. "The one from England that I mentioned." Right. His childhood friend. "He just got out of his relationship too and it...didn't go well."

"In what way?"

"...She was hurting him." He gulped and I felt his breath brush the top of my hair. "When he told me what happened, it made me think of Cindy. I got to thinking—what if we got them to meet? It might be helpful for Cindy to speak with someone who experienced a similar situation."

It hurt that I wasn't enough for her, that I could never comfort her the way I wanted to. No matter how hard I tried to help, I couldn't completely relate to her situation and understand her. How would I feel if this random guy she just met was better at helping her than I was?

I acknowledged that these thoughts were selfish, but they were honest.

That didn't mean I needed to act on them, though. I'd deal with them on my own and never let them interfere with what was right. I was older now. I had to get better at recognizing which thoughts should influence my actions.

"That might be a good idea," I said honestly. "When's he coming?" I wiped tears from my eyes before they soaked Axel's shoulder.

"Next week. I was hoping you and I could go to dinner or something and bring her along. She could meet him there," he said, dragging out each word to gauge my reaction.

I gave him a look. "Like a double date?" I clarified, getting right to the heart of the matter. I was partially joking but the mention of a date reminded me once again that I'd dodged the subject of dating Axel all month. "We talked about this, Axel. Now isn't the time for...stuff like that." I needed to focus entirely on Cindy. She needed me right now, more than Axel did. While my feelings may have swayed toward the romantic, I was still focused on my friendships first. I wouldn't be the kind of girl who ignored her friends as soon as a man appeared.

"I'm well aware," Axel said. "And I don't intend to interfere. That doesn't change my feelings, though. I'm going to pursue you regardless. Plus, it doesn't have to be a date, per se. We're just a group of friends getting together to hang out and celebrate surviving another month of school."

"Okay." This would be good for Cindy. I was sure of it. "I'll let her know and warm her up to the idea beforehand. What's your friend's name?"

"Benjamin Benedict," he said, completely serious.

I pursed my lips, trying to keep quiet, but a snort still snuck out through my nose.

Axel scoffed in pretend offense. "What's so funny?"

"Nothing, it's just..." I paused to catch my breath, wanting to burst into laughter. "That's such a stereotypical name, is all."

"Stereotypical? What kind of...Ah." He raised his chin, giving me a knowing look. "Is this about the book? It's always about the book."

"I mean, you have to admit we all have pretty stereotypical names, just like a romance novel. Cindy Annabelle. Derek Daniels. Axel Burns. And now Benjamin Benedict."

"But *your* name isn't stereotypical."

"I'm the best friend with the foreign name. It doesn't have to be as on-the-nose as your names."

"I'm not even going to dignify that comment with a response." He turned away with a roll of his eyes, making it clear he didn't agree with my silly sentiments.

I was about to say something else, enjoying the conversation and wanting to keep it going, when one of the girls we passed on the sidewalk stopped and turned around to do a double take. She was pretty with dark hair and heavy eye makeup. Her framed eyes lit up as soon as she recognized Axel.

"Axel? Is that you?" She rushed forward and wrapped both hands around his arm. "It's been so long! How are you?"

I stepped back as Axel flashed that bright, playboy grin he always used when flirting. Without skipping a beat, he started chatting with her nonchalantly like I wasn't even there. I didn't think he was doing it intentionally—flirting with girls was just what he did—but instead of rolling my eyes and ignoring the situation like I used to back in high school, I felt heat flare up in my chest. My mouth filled with acid and I took a second step back, wondering if I should just walk away.

The girl was persistently flirting as she asked him how he'd been. She kept her hands on his arm and I noted that he didn't attempt to push her away.

My stomach twisted uncomfortably. I didn't want to watch this.

Had I become possessive like Derek? Or was I just feeling disgust because Axel flirted with everyone, including me? I told him in the past that flirting should signal to someone that you like them and find them special. When he did it to everyone, it lost its charm. Up until this very moment, I had fallen for the idea that he genuinely thought I *was* special. I hadn't seen him flirt with girls in a while, after all, so I'd assumed he'd decided to settle down with one person—with me—and had given up chasing every girl he met. But this proved me wrong. I wasn't special to him. He didn't like me any more than the dozens of other girls he'd met on campus.

I was no different from the girls he led to the back of the library and promptly forgot about. The only difference was that I took a little longer to convince. His methods of seduction may have changed, but apparently the playboy Axel Burns hadn't.

His own words may have contradicted those thoughts—he'd told me he loved me—but his actions proved he didn't actually value me above the rest. Actions were the true speakers, after all, so no matter how many drunken confessions he gave, his actions proved I was just one of many. Some girls might not mind that, but I did. I wasn't going to become a single name in a never-ending list of girls.

Axel and the brunette finished their conversation after three minutes, but by that time, I was so lost in my thoughts that I missed everything they'd discussed. I just wanted to get out of there. Forget being polite. Axel wouldn't care if I left anyway.

Was the author making me think like this? No, stop! I already went over that. There was no author. There was only reality and reality dictated that I should leave.

"You ready to go?" Axel asked after rejoining me, acting as if nothing had happened.

I didn't answer for a beat. I was still wrestling with these awful, destructive thoughts. Who was in the wrong here? If liking Axel made me start feeling like this all the time, maybe it was better to get rid of these romantic sensibilities altogether.

"Are you okay?" he asked, leaning forward to study my face.

I leaned away instinctively. "I'm fine. I just want to go." It came out harsher than I expected, betraying my true feelings. Axel looked hurt for a second, then confused, then withdrawn. He opened his mouth to speak on it, but I cut him off. "I'll see you next week. Text me the location for the restaurant, okay?" Then I marched off, not caring if he called after me. I needed some time alone to think this through.

I hated how quickly my feelings could shift around him. If this was love, I wasn't sure I wanted it.

Chapter 35

I didn't speak to Axel again throughout the week. I spotted him a few times in the hallway and once in the cafeteria, but he was always with some other girl. I had hoped some time apart would make these feelings for him vanish—both the good and the bad—but instead, when I saw him smiling at those girls and letting them cozy up to him, the bile inside me got worse. It made me ache to see him again.

I didn't text him during that time, but he did need to tell me the location of the restaurant, so when he sent that text, I was forced to reply.

Hey*,** he said. ***Just an update on the restaurant thing. My friend says he's tired from jetlag so he won't be able to make it, which is a shame. I was thinking we could go just the two of us instead, then maybe in a few more days we could bring him and Cindy to a different event.

My stomach flip-flopped as I stared at the phone. I was alone in my dorm. Cindy was at one of her classes. I'd been studying but this interruption made me unable to think about anything besides what to do.

I had to reply but what should I say? I didn't want to go, especially now that I had all these icky feelings inside me. They would definitely come out if I found myself alone with Axel.

In that case, why don't we just cancel the restaurant entirely? I didn't want to see him right now. At least not until I got these jealous feelings under control so we could go back to being platonic friends.

What? Why? 🙁

I couldn't tell him the truth. He wouldn't understand. *Let's cancel. I have a lot of studying to do.*

...But I already made a reservation.

Now I was getting unreasonably annoyed. Why couldn't he just leave it alone? Every sweet thing he did only added to my inner turmoil. *Then you can take some other girl. I'm sure you won't have any trouble finding one who wants to go with you.*

There was a long pause, which made me even more nervous.

...I don't want to go with someone else, Godzilla. I want to go with you.

Now that I'd seen him in his natural habitat again, I knew he couldn't mean that. *I thought we agreed this wasn't a date!*

You know my intentions.

No, I really don't, Axel, I typed, then stared at the send button. If he wanted to date me, why did he constantly flirt with other girls? He had to know how that looked, especially after I saw him make out with seven different ones in the high school library.

I felt my heart harden as I recalled those days in the library, the annoyance and anger as I watched him cheat on his then-girl-friend. I hit send, then added, *I can never date someone I know will cheat on me.*

Another long pause. *I won't cheat on you, Zilla.*

He was doing it right now, at least in my eyes. Flirting wasn't something you just did with anybody. I would never be able to live a life married to someone who flirted with every girl he met. *We both know that's a lie. Have you already forgotten your escapades in the high school library?*

I could see him typing for quite a while, then he stopped and didn't say anything. He must have deleted what he was planning to use as a defense.

After ten minutes, I put the phone away. He wasn't going to answer. It was probably for the best.

Maybe this was all my fault. Maybe I was the one in the wrong. Should I have given him the benefit of the doubt? Sure, statistically, people who cheated once were more likely to do it again, but Axel might be different.

You aren't the exception, Zilla. You're the rule. You've always been the rule. Not even Cindy was the exception.

The horrible thoughts started to pile up, taunting me, reminding me that if he was willing to cheat on the girl from prom then he would definitely cheat on a girl like me.

The torment didn't end until my phone vibrated, making me jump. Axel had replied.

Maybe you're right, Zilla.

My heart sank. Even though he was agreeing with me, my heart had hoped he would say the opposite. *"No, I will remain loyal to you forever. You're special. You're the one. I'm a changed man."* But this wasn't a romance novel. This was real life, and in real life, people didn't change just like that. Some people never changed at all.

Can we still be friends, at least? he asked. It was the same question he'd given me numerous times. Back then, I had been glad he asked because I didn't mind staying friends.

Now, I wasn't sure if I wanted to say yes again.

...I guess.

Okay. Let's take a little time to cool down. We can discuss this with clear heads in a few days.

Right.

Now I felt awful. How many times had I said something to hurt him now? Three? Ten? He was putting up with a lot from me.

But I knew other girls would react the same way. Who would be happy to hear a guy profess his love, then see him cozy up to other girls right in front of her? I wasn't backing down. My heart would have to get used to the reality that this relationship wasn't going to happen.

"You hear that, stupid author?" I muttered. "If you are there, I'm not falling for your crappy love story. This is real life and I'm going to react like an actual human being." I no longer cared that I was giving into my delusions again. "I'm done."

Chapter 36

Right. Zilla's only response to Axel's confession had been "Right" after brutally rejecting him yet again.

Axel stared at his phone, trying to comprehend what exactly he'd done wrong. Well, he knew what he'd done wrong. He'd been doing it ever since he entered high school—refusing to get serious about a relationship because there were so many other women out there who could entertain him. Now, after cheating on every girl he'd dated and flirting with any woman he found remotely attractive, it had finally come back to bite him.

The one girl who actually made him feel more than mild interest had pushed him away, and he was pretty sure it was for good this time.

Axel was so preoccupied with his thoughts that he didn't even notice his best friend Benjamin enter his bedroom. He'd come from the shared dorm's living room where he'd been taking a nap.

"What's up?" Benjamin asked, his English accent far more distinct than Axel's. His black hair was rumpled and even after running a hand through it, it didn't do much good. His brown skin had a few lines across it, the result of sleeping on a wrinkly pillow on an equally uncomfortable couch. "Did a girl just chew you out for cheating again?" he asked, his sing-song tone a result of seeing this exact event play out dozens of times before, albeit through a video stream or phone call. The sad thing was, Ben was right, but it was a vastly different dilemma this time.

"Yeah," Axel replied, the word coming out as a long sigh.

A look of concern crossed Ben's face, and he took a seat on Axel's bed beside a pile of dirty laundry. Axel hadn't bothered cleaning it up since he was too busy worrying about Zilla. Now it didn't matter how sloppy he was. She wasn't going to be part of his future anymore, so why bother being tidy?

"Okay," Ben said slowly, gesturing for Axel to keep talking. "Then why do you look so down about it? It's not like you care. What's different this time?" He made a loud "hmming" sound as he thought about it, then snapped his fingers. "She insulted your looks! You're a vain guy, so she must have called you ugly or commented on your dumb hairstyle. Oh boy, whatever she said must have been the truth because—"

"No," Axel said, resembling a droopy-eared dog. "It's not because of something dumb like that."

"Then what?" Ben waited. Axel could tell Ben was hoping it was a more personal reason. He'd started to change in the last year or two, caring more about morality and loyalty than messing around with women. Axel knew Ben would be thrilled that he had actually fallen for someone this time. He'd view it as the first step toward positive, lifelong change.

"It's because—" Axel sighed. "Because it's a girl I genuinely like."

Ben gave him a funny look, then realized he was serious and gasped, making the intake of breath extra long for added effect.

Both of them were fans of acting dramatically, sometimes for fun and sometimes in a failed attempt to brighten the mood. The two had been as close as brothers from the age of two so they'd begun to act the same over time. The only difference between them was in appearance. While Axel was the flashy, handsome boy with light hair and eyes, Ben was exceedingly plain with dark features. Their differences never bothered them, and Ben's flirty personality made up for his looks, but they still looked vastly different on the outside. Until they went their separate ways at eight years old, they were an immensely popular pair in their middle school for lighting up the room with their jokes and chatter.

"You actually felt, dare I say it, feelings?" Ben asked, dramatically raising a hand to the sky as though a miracle had occurred. Perhaps it had. "Axel has felt stirrings in his heart. I never thought I'd see the day."

Axel stayed slouched in his chair, facing away from his friend. He wasn't in the mood for jokes right now.

After a full minute of sullen silence, Ben finally dropped his hands and lowered his voice. "I came all the way from England to visit you and now you won't even be honest with me. Let's be up front here. Tell me what happened."

That was all it took to convince Axel. He hadn't been able to tell anyone about this situation with Xiang, mainly because he hadn't taken his relationship with her seriously until now. He hadn't realized the true extent of his feelings and how much he cared about her until she sent that text dismissing him from her life.

So, Axel told Ben everything about Zilla, from their first meeting at prom, to his choice of university, to Derek, and now, finally, her angry text saying she could never love him the way he was starting to love her.

He also explained why, instead of fighting to win her over yet again, he was giving up. Rather than beg her to forgive his cheating past and promise to do better, he decided she was right and had conceded.

"I'm not bothered that she wants me to give up my flirting habits," Axel finished after giving Ben the summary, trying to skew it in favor of Zilla so Ben wouldn't have a biased view. Ben wasn't the type to hold grudges—he didn't even hate his ex-girlfriend for abusing him—but Axel wanted Ben to view Zilla as positively as he did.

"Then what was it that finally made you give up?" Ben asked, all teasing gone. He was leaning forward on the bed, his forehead wrinkled. His former girlfriend had made him more serious about real romantic relationships, even though that specific one ended up turning abusive. Despite the negatives, the experience had showed Ben that he wanted more than emotionless flings with girls. He wanted something real and lasting, or so he claimed.

"It was because..." Axel allowed his voice to trail off as he leaned back in his chair, attempting to get his thoughts straight. "It's because she could be right. I might cheat on her someday. As soon as—" He grit his teeth, hating the recent memory. "As soon as she sent that text saying she didn't want to date me, my first instinct was to immediately text some other girl."

Ben let the silence hang in the air for a moment.

"But you wouldn't have done it...Would you?"

He wouldn't have, but if the temptation came again, maybe he would. He couldn't be sure. This was the first time he actually felt motivated to ignore the temptation.

That was why he didn't argue against Zilla's assessment. She hadn't been wrong about his habits. He was tempted, in that moment, to cheat and run to someone else when things got tough.

"That silence is all the answer I needed." Ben tilted his head, acknowledging with his frown just how awful this was. Then he steeled his expression and leaned forward even more, spreading his hands out to show that it was time to search for solutions. "You really like this girl, right?"

"I might even love her," Axel acknowledged miserably.

"Right, love. And you don't want to cheat on her, right? Not really. You seem pretty disgusted by the thought of it."

"I don't want to cheat on her," Axel affirmed. But he had been tempted all the same. He even went to the contact list on his phone and started scrolling, searching for some girl to substitute for Zilla. It had happened so quickly and easily. His mind had barely caught up with his hand. He did manage to stop himself, but what if that self-control failed next time? He'd been right on the edge of giving in—

"Then here's what I think, speaking from personal experience," Ben said, interrupting Axel's thoughts. "You've been chasing girls all your life, right? You always seek out short term relationships, never taking anything seriously, never caring. I should know. We were cut from the same cloth."

Axel nodded. Ben wasn't really looking for confirmation anyway. He knew Axel well enough.

"So, you've formed a habit of cheating, flirting, getting with anybody. You did it when you were single *and* in relationships. So, how are you going to break that habit?"

Axel shrugged, not sure what kind of answer Ben wanted.

"You have to start practicing self-control. The key to doing that long term is doing it *all the time*, even when you're not dating anyone."

All the time? Even right now? "So, you're telling me to be loyal, even when there's nobody to be loyal to?" It sounded dumb.

"You developed the habit of cheating and sleeping around while you were single. Habits aren't immediately broken when you step into a relationship. You have to build that habit now, before you even meet your partner. Otherwise, those tendencies will follow you around and they'll eventually make you lose the right girl when she does come along."

"So you're saying I should be alone...all the time..." Axel didn't like the sound of that. He couldn't imagine going through his teen years like Ben suggested. It felt unnatural...but then again, it was all he'd ever known. Besides, when he was younger, he never believed he'd actually fall in love.

"Do you like this girl or not?"

"...I do."

"Then you'll have to build those habits now. If you ever convince her to date you, those habits will hopefully be gone by then. If they aren't, at least you'll have built up enough immunity to help you resist and stay loyal to her, like you wanted. Plus, if she sees you actively try to stop flirting and messing around with girls, maybe she'll have a change of heart and take you back."

Axel leaned back in his chair and gave it some thought. He still detested himself for thinking about cheating on Zilla or replacing her. It felt like his body had moved on all on its own...but he couldn't place the blame on his body. Ben might be right. It was a mindset that needed changing, not a relationship status.

"Statistically," Ben added, as was fitting for a psychology major like him, "the more partners someone has before a relationship, the more likely they are to cheat. People with over five past sexual partners are twice as likely to cheat, with a twenty-five percent—"

"You don't need to give me the numbers, Ben."

"I'm just saying. You've already screwed up that last part, but if you actually put your mind to it, you might be able to change."

"What, like you?" Axel asked, rolling his head toward Ben in annoyance. His best friend had started attending a church after his breakup and had supposedly changed his ways, but he still ended up dating a girl who took advantage of him. Plus... "You weren't much better than me at one point."

Ben shrugged. "I won't lie to you; I'm still tempted too. But I can thankfully admit that the longer I stick to my guns, the easier it gets. This might work for you, or it might not. But if you really love this girl or intend to get married to someone someday, I think it's best to start practicing now rather than later when you've run out of time."

Axel frowned, fiddling with his phone. "Well, she's not talking to me anymore, so—"

"So it's a great time to put those new habits into action. *Show* her you've given up on hook-up culture, rather than just *telling* her," Ben finished, then smiled cheekily. "Besides, that nap helped my jet lag immensely, so I might be able to meet your girl for dinner after all, and her friend, of course."

"I told you, she didn't want—"

"But *I* do. If she's as overprotective of her best friend as you said, she'll show up as long as her friend does. So, give me the best friend's number and I'll arrange it myself."

Axel saw where this was going and tapped his nose in a conspiratorial way. Ben planned to invite Cindy and if Cindy accepted, Zilla had to go.

Axel was about to give in, then he thought better of it and groaned. "That's not a good idea. You might creep out Cindy. She has no idea who you are."

Ben flashed a second devious smile. "Then I think it's time I—" He paused to show Axel an unimpressive smolder. "—turn on the charm."

Axel smirked, unwilling to compliment his friend's overconfidence. "Yeah, good luck with that, Benny."

"Don't use that name!" Ben shouted, back to his regular antics. "It's Ben, now!"

"Sorry, Benjamin Benedict."

Ben glared at him.

Axel continued smirking. "Ben Ben."

"If you say it like that again, I won't help you get the girl!"

"...Noted."

Chapter 37

The following weekend, I planned a shopping spree for me and Cindy. I needed to keep myself distracted. If I stayed at home watching movies or reading, my mind would wander toward Axel. I didn't want that hot, searing jealousy to leap through my chest again. It felt awful and made me feel like a jerk.

When Saturday morning came around, I knocked on the bathroom door, ready to invite Cindy out to the mall. I was expecting her to be in there for an hour. Weekends were her chance to sing and contemplate life in the shower until she was red in the face. However, to my great surprise, two knocks in, Cindy threw the door open and walked out with her hair styled and makeup done. She didn't normally put on more than mascara during the weekends. What was going on?

"Perfect timing," she told me, flashing a grin that had become rare ever since Derek left. "I was just about to wake you up."

Why? "Are you going somewhere?" Cindy hadn't mentioned any weekend plans and if there were, she would have invited me. She wasn't the type to go places by herself.

I normally would have been thrilled that she was finally planning things on her own, even if it was without me, but it was strange that she hadn't at least told me about it. We were roommates, after all.

Cindy tilted her head, confused. "What do you mean? I thought you were coming too."

"Where?" I hadn't asked her to go shopping yet. The idea only popped into my head an hour ago.

"To have breakfast with Axel and his friend. I thought you two arranged it." Cindy studied me suspiciously. "Why are you acting oblivious? Is there something I don't know? Or was I about to get scammed by a stranger?" Now she was on edge, worried it might be a trap. If I didn't intervene soon, she'd think Derek had returned from the States and was planning to kidnap her again, luring her away with a fake invite.

Grabbing her hands, which were starting to shake, I shook my head. "I was planning to go out, but Axel and I got in a fight so I thought it wasn't happening." I frowned, thinking it through. "Maybe his friend didn't hear about the cancellation. Was he the one who contacted you or was it Axel?"

"It was the friend. His name's Ben."

"Right." I turned away, biting my lip. I couldn't meet Axel's friend at a time like this. It would be beyond awkward, for both me and Cindy. "Can you cancel? Axel and I aren't exactly on speaking terms."

"I could—" Cindy paused. Her phone had just buzzed in her pocket. "That might be him." She pulled it out and turned it on so both of us could see the screen.

Hey! I'm here a little early. It was from the Ben person. Dang it! Too late to cancel now. It was rude enough to be late but cancelling when he was already there was beyond inconsiderate. My parents would be ashamed of me if I did.

I grimaced and released Cindy. "I'll go get ready," I whispered, already dreading this. "Give me twenty minutes."

"I'll tell him," Cindy called after me. She actually sounded excited for once, solidifying the reality that I'd have to go through with this whether I liked it or not. The only consolation was that Axel might not be there.

"Axel can keep him entertained until we arrive," Cindy added.

Scratch that. Axel was there too. Why had he decided to go even though he knew I didn't want to see him? This was going to be horrible.

Chapter 38

As Cindy and I got off the bus and approached the outlet mall where Axel and Ben were waiting, I tugged down my shorts for the fourth time that morning. They kept riding up. Despite looking the best in the mirror, they ended up being the most uncomfortable. I normally wouldn't have bothered wearing them, but despite still being pissed at Axel, part of me was desperate to look good in front of him. It didn't matter, since most of his female friends were better looking than me anyway, but regardless, the urge never abated.

Man, I was really turning back into a superficial person, wasn't I? I used to never care what people thought of my looks...well, I still didn't. It only mattered when it came to *him* and the book.

Cindy was humming as she walked, her steps a little bouncier than before. For the entire week after her near kidnapping, she had dragged her heels and zoned out. Now she was the one leading the way past various shops, restaurants, and people.

We were headed for a coffee shop known for its sweet, unique blends and small-business vibes. I was glad it was coffee instead of a full meal. I could get through a coffee in twenty minutes, then politely excuse myself and drag Cindy along behind me. I'd only have to stare into Axel's hurt eyes for a short time before getting out of there.

Unfortunately, when Cindy opened the front door and entered, there was a long line at the counter. Instead of saving a spot in line for us when they arrived earlier, Axel and his friend had decided to save us a corner table instead. They were seated there now, waiting for us while chatting with each other. If they had just saved a spot in the long, snaking line, this date would have gone a lot quicker.

I huffed and tried to distract myself by studying Axel's best friend instead. This Ben person was cute, and he was waving his hands around as he spoke, making the story he was telling animated and somewhat charming. But of course, compared to Axel, he looked plain. His hair wasn't styled—it naturally curled over the top of his forehead and tips of his ears with no shape. His facial features were plain too. He wasn't ugly but nothing about him particularly stood out.

There I was, being superficial again. I thought I had improved this year. While I always focused on appearances growing up, it was in the context of everything being a book setting. That had given me an excuse to do it freely. Now I had no reason other than my own shallowness to judge people. It was time to put an end to it.

Ben spotted us first, since Axel had his back to us, and he paused to point us out to Axel before waving, unsure if we were the girls he had come to meet. That was when Axel turned around and we made eye contact. For a split second, I saw hurt flash across his eyes as he and I stared at each other. Then those emotions vanished and he pasted on a perfect smile, calling our names and gesturing for us to take a seat.

Cindy waved, then pulled me forward so we could join them. I experienced déjà vu as I followed her. In our last year of high school, *I* had been the one instigating a seating arrangement between her and Derek in a fast-food restaurant. Now she was the one doing the instigating. I never imagined our roles flipping like this.

After we introduced ourselves, Ben suggested he and Cindy get in line to order drinks. Cindy looked at me—knowing I wouldn't want to be left alone with Axel, who hadn't spoken yet—but I motioned for her to go ahead. We were already stuck in this mess. No point dragging things out and making it even more unpleasant.

I watched silently as Ben escorted Cindy to the line, entirely leading the conversation and never letting his smile drop.

"So," Axel said once they were gone. "What do you think of him?"

I studied Ben a bit longer, glad Axel had stuck to a neutral conversation starter. "He seems nice. I haven't seen enough of him to make a judgement yet." I noticed that Ben was immediately attentive to Cindy, acting like a gentleman and gesturing for her to go ahead of him in line, then discussing the menu with her. She seemed to enjoy letting someone else lead.

"He's changed a lot since I last saw him a few years ago," Axel commented, half of his mouth quirking up from childhood memories. "He used to be a ladies' man until he settled down."

"Settled down? You told me he broke up with his girlfriend. Wasn't she..." I clamped my mouth shut, not wanting to bring up abuse and spoil the mood. It would be awful if Ben and Cindy returned and overheard us discussing it.

Axel nodded somberly, not voicing it either. "But he's trying to turn over a new leaf."

"Well, that's good." I leaned away, not wanting to say something like, *"You could learn a thing or two."* Not only would that be unnecessarily cruel and biting, but it would make me a hypocrite. I wasn't perfect either and Axel knew it.

The conversation drifted off after that. I wasn't giving Axel much to work with.

As Axel waited for Ben's return, he started picking apart a napkin, forming a little pile of shavings under his hands. He didn't try to say anything else, though his brow was furrowed like he wanted to.

Cindy and Ben were halfway through the line now.

"How's Cindy doing?" Axel asked finally. The question was repetitive, but I was more than happy to discuss it.

"I think she's doing better." I hated to admit it in some ways, but it was true. "I haven't seen her this lively in a while. Honestly, I'm...glad we ended up coming."

When I glanced at Axel, he was smiling, genuinely happy for her. Then he gestured toward his best friend. "Like I said, I figured Ben and Cindy could become good friends. I've always thought they'd get along, even before Ben said he was coming."

"I agree. As long as he's a good guy, that is."

"Oh, he is. Trust me. He's a much better man than me."

I couldn't help smiling at his modesty. "You're not that bad," I said, making him turn to me in surprise, playfully shocked that I had complimented him. "At being a friend, that is," I added quickly.

"Right." There it was—the dreaded pain in his eyes, like he was a puppy I'd just kicked. "Sorry about that. I..." He grimaced, like he didn't want to say this next part. "I'll try to become someone you're more comfortable with."

What did he mean by that? Was he still talking about a dating relationship or just being friends? I refused to prod him further. I didn't want to have that conversation yet. "Okay."

"I want to become the kind of man you'd...enjoy spending your life with," he added. Now I definitely knew he was talking about dating. He still wanted to pursue me it seemed, but knew I wasn't comfortable with cheaters and playboys.

He sounded like he meant what he said, at least, but words meant nothing if actions didn't back them up. I wasn't inclined to believe him. Besides, I'd already rejected him. This wasn't just me saying *no* stubbornly either. This was me admitting that we weren't a good match regardless of our feelings. No amount of time or discussion would change that.

But sitting there, next to him, my heart betrayed me. I *wanted* him to change for me and I wanted to change too. I wanted to become someone who could stand by his side and not feel inadequate. I also wanted to feel confident that he actually loved me and me alone.

When had I become such an insecure romantic?

Our friends arrived with a tray of drinks and Ben handed them out, imitating a waiter to get a chuckle out of us. Then he led the conversation, talking about what was different here in Canada and how our accents didn't match. I personally didn't notice a difference between Canadian and American accents, but he apparently had a better ear for it.

Throughout the conversation, I noticed Cindy slowly warming up to Ben. She started by giving him and everyone else nervous smiles, then when Ben cracked enough jokes, she started laughing loudly. She rarely did that unless she was comfortable. I'd never seen her warm up to someone that fast, not even Axel.

I caught myself glancing across the table at Axel as the "double date" continued. I couldn't help it. The sight of him still made me feel warm and fuzzy inside.

When he caught me staring, I played it off as intentional, following the stare with a nod toward Ben and Cindy. Did he think they were getting along a bit too well? I accentuated this by raising an eyebrow. Axel just chuckled silently and gave me a subtle shrug so our silent conversation wouldn't be discovered.

I focused on Ben again and noticed how attentive he was to Cindy, even in the group conversation. He always looked at her first after making a joke. He wasn't as obvious about his interest as Axel was, but the signs were all there.

Was this Ben fellow interested in Cindy romantically? That didn't sit right with me, not yet anyway. She was fresh out of a relationship and had just met the guy. Sure, he seemed nice, but it was too soon.

Derek's voice entered my head at that moment, telling me to lay off and leave Cindy alone. It wasn't my right to pry. I shouldn't turn into a mother hen.

But leaving things alone had been the reason Cindy got hurt by Derek. I could have interfered back then and chose not to. I shouldn't make that mistake again.

I looked down at my lap, caught between a rock and a hard place. I didn't look up again until Axel called my name, drawing me back into the conversation and looking concerned. I wasn't surprised he'd been able to read my thoughts. Trying to hide them, I hopped back into the conversation. The group had drifted into a discussion about Ben potentially getting a job here. I wasn't sure how I felt about that either.

By the time the coffee cups were empty, forty minutes had passed and most of my unease had faded. I even said yes when Ben invited us to a movie the following weekend. I didn't realize that meant more time with Axel until we parted ways.

"So," I asked Cindy as we headed into a clothing store near the coffee shop. It would be a waste to come all this way and not go shopping like I planned. "What do you think of Ben?"

"He seems...kind," Cindy said, frowning.

"Then why are you frowning?"

"Nothing, it's just...he was really nice," she said.

Ah. I knew what it was. She was starting to like him, ever so slightly, and was just as confused about it as me. Her last relationship just ended and, if I remembered correctly, his did too. I would feel odd if I was in her situation and immediately met a new guy who piqued my interest.

"Let's just hang out as friends for now," I said to relieve her stress.

"Oh!" Cindy brightened. "That reminds me. About you and Axel—"

"Nothing to tell," I said before she could start prying.

"Oh." Her face dropped but I brushed it off with a laugh.

"Let's not talk about boys anymore. I've had enough of them for today."

That made Cindy laugh, since we both knew talking about boys was turning into one of our favorite things to do. But she went along with it, thankfully. She knew me just as well as Axel and could tell when I needed a break from real life. This was one of those times.

Chapter 39

That coffee double date was one of the best and worst things to happen that month. It was great because it helped me and Axel break through the awkwardness of my official rejection. It was also great because it allowed Ben to join our group and help us feel like normal college students again, rather than people trying to recover from an encounter with a weird, possessive ex-boyfriend.

However, it also meant I had to continue encountering Axel, being constantly reminded of how much I actually liked him despite knowing I shouldn't. Following these romantic feelings would end in disaster. Our personalities weren't compatible. That was all there was to it.

...But then I would stumble across Axel assisting Cindy with her studies, encouraging her as she stressed over an upcoming exam. That spark of love would be rekindled and I'd be back to square one.

So, the reunification of our friend group, plus the new addition, had its positives, but it also made things harder for me in the long run.

After his holiday ended, Ben decided he was going to officially move in with Axel and work remotely so he could spend more time in Canada. Their roommate arrangement wasn't completely above-board, since you weren't supposed to stay in a dorm when you weren't a student, but when the room was about to be inspected, Ben would come hang out with me and Cindy instead. Or rather, he sat next to me and spent the whole hour chatting nonstop with Cindy. They got along really well. In just a few weeks, Ben managed to peel away Cindy's shy exterior and reveal the hyper, geeky girl underneath that only I used to know.

The longer I listened to that pair talk, the more they had in common. Ben liked anime and Cindy liked the books that came with it. Those romantic comics were something she'd latched onto during her time recovering from Derek. I had worried reading cute stories about romance and happy endings would remind her about how poorly her own relationship went, but it seemed to heal her instead, so I never commented on it.

Ben also enjoyed that form of entertainment, though he preferred the action and comedy genres to the sweet, romantic ones. While I studied with headphones on in the corner of my room, they would chat about what they'd recently read or watched.

Their conversations sometimes continued for hours on end, so when I needed a moment of peace and quiet, I'd head to the library or a university café to clear my head. I appreciated Ben's company immensely, to be sure, but that didn't change the fact that I preferred studying alone.

It was on one of those days, when I'd escaped to a café with my textbooks, that Axel found me.

I was on my third trip to my favorite coffee shop, nestled right in the middle of a school building with a lot of foot traffic. It was while I was sitting there, bored out of my mind by my mandatory reading, that Axel spotted me at my lone table. He had been walking past with some buddies of his but when he saw me, he decided I needed a break from studying and marched toward me with a goodbye to his friends and a shouted greeting to me.

Since I did need a break, I welcomed the interruption, even though I feared the awkwardness that might arise between us.

"I thought that was you," Axel said as I closed my textbook and looked up at him. "Do you mind having a little extra company?"

I shrugged and pointed at the menu behind the café counter. "I recommend a coffee. Their other drinks aren't that good."

"Noted." Looking relieved that I hadn't immediately sent him away, he trotted off to order a black coffee and returned a minute later with it in hand. Then he sat across from me, talking about a potluck the gaming club was holding the following week. He led the conversation from the potluck to games, then anime, then Ben and Cindy's fascination with it. By the time we reached that fourth topic, I was chatting away without a second thought.

"I can't understand how a show about turning into slime can fill two hours of conversation," I said to him twenty minutes into our own discussion. He was listening to me vent without a word of interruption, the tops of his lips quirking up in amusement as I allowed myself to rant ceaselessly.

I was both exhausted and ecstatic about Ben and Cindy's bonding. Part of me was a little jealous, seeing a relationship unfold that I wanted for myself but couldn't have with a good conscience. "Then an hour later, they were discussing the use of tanukis in romantic literature."

"Tanukis?"

"Little raccoon things." I sighed and leaned back in my chair. "I'm glad they're getting along and having fun, but sometimes I wish he'd just ask her on a date so they could discuss it in private. There's a limit to how much manga discussion I can take."

"Ben's trying to be respectful when it comes to the girl he likes, so he's taking his time," Axel explained quietly, sounding proud.

"Wait. Say that again," I said, making sure I didn't misunderstand. *The girl he likes?* Ben had only been here for a few weeks, a month at most. Had he already decided to pursue Cindy?

"He's trying to respect—"

"Is Ben seriously trying to date Cindy?"

"He is, though he hasn't made that clear to her yet. He knows she's been through a lot." Axel tilted his head and looked me in the eye, hinting that he was doing the same to me.

"Does he genuinely like her?" I asked, ignoring his look. "Or is he the type to just pursue a girl for a bit, then leave for England after he's had his fun?" I no longer cared about being overprotective, as long as it was within reason. If it didn't interfere with Cindy's life and kept her safe, I was happy to at least investigate the man in question.

"I think he does," Axel said. "Like I said, he's a good guy. I mean it."

"Hmm." I leaned away, my brain trying to compartmentalize Ben as it always did. If Ben was a character in a book, what role would he play? "He's a joker," I continued. "Jokers are—"

"Godzilla," Axel warned and I froze. I was judging people by their stereotypical traits again.

"Jokers can have a lot of merits," I finished, glad he caught the temptation and nipped it in the bud. "And from what I've seen, he doesn't seem like the type who will break her heart."

"Agreed." Axel nodded, raising an eyebrow.

"But he might not be the right one for her," I added, needing to bring at least a touch of caution back. "I'll wait a little longer before

I make a final decision about his character. I'll need time to get to know him better."

Derek had checked all the storybook boxes and that was why I let all his red flags slide. Now I had learned my lesson.

"Good, good." Axel was clearly thinking the same. I hoped he knew I was making an effort to be rid of our book theory. "Unless he's hiding some secret personality that I've yet to see in over ten years, then I can vouch for him."

"Yes, because you're *so* trustworthy," I joked. Luckily, he knew I wasn't being genuine and played along, eager to start a battle of sarcastic banter.

"I'll have you know, Godzilla, that my mother says I'm—"

"Axel!"

We both turned as yet another woman I hadn't met came running up to us from the crowded walkway. This one had pretty, curly brown hair and wasn't wearing makeup, though her face was so beautiful that she didn't need it. She had arched eyebrows and clear skin that shone.

I straightened as she pulled up a chair next to Axel and sat without asking for permission to join. Déjà vu struck me and I willed any jealousy to die out. It wouldn't help the situation. Plus, I no longer planned to date Axel anyway.

"I can't believe I caught you today," the newcomer said, then paused and acknowledged me. "I'm Emma, nice to meet you."

"Nice to meet you," I said quietly, letting things play out.

"Emma's becoming a teacher too," Axel explained, helping me join the conversation. "She's heading to China a year ahead of me."

"Ah." I didn't know he was planning to go to China specifically. When had he decided that?

I was tempted to say nothing and let them chat, but my conscience reminded me to actually be nice. I had promised myself I would improve when it came to interacting with strangers and, so far, I had barely done anything outside the club. "Do you speak any languages besides English?"

The girl grinned at me, then rattled off something I knew was in Mandarin but couldn't understand, partly because of her pronunciation and also because I hadn't spoken Mandarin since I was a preteen. My parents always communicated in English and we hadn't visited China in years so I'd forgotten most of it.

I smiled back and had to sadly admit, in Mandarin, that I could barely speak the language even though I was half-Chinese.

The girl showed her pearly whites again, proud that she understood what I said, then she switched back to English with a heavy Canadian accent. "I'm still studying so I'm not too good at it yet," she admitted shyly, showing a new side of herself. I felt my own heart blossom with warmth. A moment ago, this girl had felt like a rival, but now she was a kindred spirit.

"You just reminded me I should study it again," I said, beaming.

"And that would make it easy for me to learn too," Axel added, then redirected the conversation away from me to discuss the class he shared with the girl.

For a good ten seconds, I was listening to them with a smile, then I snapped back to my senses and remembered what happened the last time Axel chatted with a girl. I was honestly expecting him to start acting like he did last time, leaning toward her and showing off a bright, flirtatious smile while making constant jokes.

But instead, he was giving her a polite grin and wasn't leaning in. He made a few jokes, but they felt friendly rather than flirtatious, and the girl started reacting the same way, mirroring him.

That felt…strange. It was so unlike how he normally acted. Was something wrong? Maybe he wasn't attracted to this girl or she had a boyfriend…though that hadn't held Axel back during high school.

As their conversation wrapped up, I leaned back in my chair and started sipping what remained of my now cold coffee. Had Axel finally made an effort to change? Or was this just a coincidence?

My brain, or at least the romantic half, immediately started forming plans about what this could mean for our relationship. If he stopped being a flirt, maybe we could make this dating thing work.

No, he was still a cheater in the past. I would never be able to rest if I dated him and especially if we got married. The paranoia would never leave. But maybe he'd made an effort to get rid of that habit. Anyone could change if they put their mind to it.

No. I doubted that.

Well, actually, I couldn't be sure.

On and on it went, fighting like an angel and a devil on each shoulder, though I couldn't tell which was which.

I was in the midst of this internal debate when the girl Emma walked away with a wave and Axel turned back to me. I could have sworn his smile changed when he faced me. It was brighter and happier, reserved and unique, designed especially for me and no one else.

No. That was probably just wishful thinking.

"So, where were we?" Axel asked.

"Ben." I gulped, hoping he didn't notice how nervous I'd become.

"Right. Since you brought that up, I'd like to mention something he told me yesterday." Thankfully, Axel seemed oblivious about my feelings for once.

"Oh?"

"Ben said he wanted to visit our gaming club."

He said *our* club. Cute.

"So I figured, since Ben's coming and it's his first time, why don't you invite Cindy too? She might be more willing to come if she's not the only new person attending."

"You make a good point." I'd asked Cindy to come before but she'd let her social anxiety get the better of her. This might offer the perfect solution. Plus, I was pretty sure she at least liked Ben as a friend. She was far more likely to say yes if it meant spending more time with him. "I'll ask her."

I didn't comment on what had just transpired between Axel and me.

Maybe there was hope for us yet.

Then again, maybe not.

But, if he did end up changing long term, I would know without needing to hear it from his mouth. His actions would prove it. Now all I could do was wait and watch, as I always did. The only difference was that now I had hope in my heart again, pushing away the negative doubts that had persisted all month long.

Chapter 40

"Are you sure I won't fall behind?" Cindy asked as I led her down one of the snaking university paths toward the gaming club building. "I've heard board games have a lot of rules and they can get confusing. I don't want to drag my team down—"

"You don't need to worry about that. The girls aren't competitive and if there are teams, which isn't that common, you can work together with me," I replied, running my hands over my wrinkled white t-shirt as I walked. There wasn't an ironing board here and I was nervous about looking rumpled in front of Axel. "I knew nothing about games when I joined and I haven't had much of a problem. Besides, you play video games occasionally, right?"

"Yes, but just racing and farming games. Nothing crazy," she whispered nervously, as though that was something to be embarrassed about.

"That's exactly what they play in the club." I was pretty sure we'd already gone over this a month ago but times had changed since then. "You'll be fine. I'll teach you all the board game rules and I'm sure Axel will teach you how to play the video games too."

Sure enough, as we entered the same gaming room I'd attended every week for the entire school year, we saw that Axel was already there. He was seated on the couch in front of the huge monitor and was joined by three other boys. They were playing a racing game and, judging by the look of defeat on Axel's face and the cheers of his friends, he had just lost miserably.

The Dungeons and Dragons table was full, as always, but there were two other board game tables with a few empty seats I could snag. Cindy could either join me or Axel. She'd be fine either way.

"Zilla!" Axel waved at me, welcoming the distraction from his miserable loss, then shouted Cindy's name too. "Do you like video games?" he added, keeping the vibe of the room upbeat with his boundless energy.

I saw Cindy calm down a little as she looked up at the gaming screen. She must have recognized the game or at least something similar to it. I immediately relaxed too. This meant she'd settle down easily and not regret finally accepting my invitation.

"Yes, I like them," she said.

Axel held out the controller for her. "Then you can take my place. I can teach you how to play," he said.

"You're better off learning on your own. If anyone needs teaching, it's him," one of the boys said, laughing as he pointed at the leaderboard. Axel was comfortably in the bottom, far below the rest.

Cindy glanced at me, still worried, but I ushered her forward to join Axel, who immediately gave up his seat on the couch so she could take it. Then he helped her learn the controls.

I watched as the next race began and she got the hang of it quickly. Axel started by telling her what to do, sitting right beside her and pointing things out excitedly, but then he let her go when he realized she knew what she was doing. I clapped and cheered loudly when she came in fourth place at the end of the race, leagues ahead of Axel's score.

Once I saw Cindy laughing, I knew she was going to be just fine and headed off to join another game.

"Zilla!" Some of the girls greeted me warmly as I approached their table. "We thought you weren't going to make it."

"And miss you explaining the rules for the fifth time?" I joked as I took a seat, feeling quite pleased with how things were turning out.

The girls laughed, then the "dealer" started handing out cards. I took mine with a small grin, feeling almost completely comfortable here. Everyone was so nice and they were easy to get along with. They didn't mind my sarcasm either, which used to be a rarity in high school.

Ben arrived a few minutes into our game and, after greeting a few people who were presumably his and Axel's roommates, he joined me at my table.

"Give us one more minute," I told him so he'd stay in the loop. "You can join us in the next round."

"Great. I'll learn by watching you." Ben leaned forward, like a child watching ants travel along the ground.

As the cards were handed out and rules explained yet again for Ben's sake, I noticed that Ben kept glancing at Cindy throughout the instructions, making me swell with an odd sense of pride as I saw the look in his eyes. I was convinced he realized just how adorable and kind-hearted Cindy was, which I already knew. It felt nice to see another person share such admiration for her.

However, as I turned to watch her and Axel debate over who should play the next round, a familiar and haunting feeling swung back into my chest. Watching them sit right next to each other, sharing the controller, I became overwhelmed with jealousy again. But this time it felt much more ugly and heavy, because this wasn't directed at some random girl on the street. This was aimed at Cindy, my favorite person in the world. That was never how things were supposed to be. Cindy and I were never meant to be rivals, ever, both *in* the book and outside of it. Cindy was my priority over any man. I should never feel a single pang of annoyance when I saw her with someone else.

I clenched the cards in my hands a little too tight as I watched Axel lean toward her to point out a secret button combo she could use. He was speaking like a child describing his favorite toy during show and tell. They both looked so happy, unaware of how close they were.

Holding my breath, I forced myself to dismiss the feeling. I could never allow it to grow or dictate my actions. It wasn't right. I could never allow my jealousy to show through.

When I glanced at Ben, I didn't see that same jealousy or longing in his eyes that I was sure I had in my own. Was he just that confident in himself? Or could he read Axel better than me?

"Then you write the definition you think would fit—" The girl explaining the rules, Titania, huffed and lowered her cards. "Ben, I'm not going to explain the rules twice, you know." She snapped her fingers to force Ben to look at her instead of Cindy, then poked my shoulder. "And Zilla too? What has you two so distracted?"

"Sorry, I was zoning out," I said quickly, embarrassed about getting caught. When I turned back around to face the rest of the table, I could tell by their expressions that they knew I'd been staring at Axel. Some of the girls already assumed Axel and I were dating, while other presumed I had an unrequited love. No matter how many times I insisted neither of those things were true, I'd still receive doubtful looks.

I refused to look over my shoulder again as we played cards. I wouldn't give these girls any more ammo to add to their misconceptions about my and Axel's relationship, even though I didn't mind their teasing.

Ben won the game, surprisingly, despite missing half the instructions, and he made sure to jokingly rub it in Axel's face even though Axel wasn't even playing with us.

The rest of our club hour went really well. We played a few more board games, I tried playing a fighting video game against Cindy and lost, and Ben became the life of the "party" with his jokes and ridiculous singing as he danced across the Dungeons and Dragons table. By the end, this felt more like a comedy club than a gaming one.

When it came time to leave, everyone was eager to give Ben a friendly send-off. I was sure he'd return next week. If he didn't, there'd be a riot.

Ben walked Cindy out, keeping his hands respectfully at his sides as they left, while Axel and I trailed after them with a good twenty-foot gap to give them some space. I was sure Ben appreciated it.

"I'm really glad they came," Axel said, once again sounding like a proud father as he watched Ben regale Cindy with some new story I couldn't hear. "I think they had a lot of fun."

"I'm sure of it," I said, smiling fondly at the memory of Cindy winning the race at the end of the night. She had cheered, despite being so shy at the start. Axel had really helped her warm up to everyone else. He was a good influence.

...Part of me didn't like the thought of that. I silenced that part of my brain as soon as the thought crossed my mind.

I glanced at Axel, trying to sort out these feelings, but my heart skipped a beat when I caught him already staring back at me. He only looked away after a quick second, not acting embarrassed about getting caught. My worries about him being with Cindy had been pointless.

Now that I thought about it, he hadn't acted flirty with *anyone* in the club today. Most of his conversations with the girls had been fruitlessly flirty until now, giving the occasional flattering comment or suggestive wink. This month, though, things had gone down a different path. He still chatted and joked around but the vibe felt different.

"What is it?" Axel asked. "Am I in trouble for something?"

I gulped, then quickly recovered. "I don't know. Did you *do* something I should be worried about?" I deflected jokingly.

"I don't think so, not unless you count losing every single game today," he replied, waiting for me to react before laughing at his own joke. I scoffed as I always did, and that apparently counted, so he chuckled a second after.

"Cindy whooped your butt," I replied with a smile, then faced forward again. As soon as I did, I froze and grabbed Axel's arm to stop him from walking. "I think I just heard Ben say something about a date."

"Really?" Axel turned his head so his ear faced the couple. "We shouldn't have stopped. We'll be out of earshot if they keep walking."

"Hush." I softly slapped his arm, then took a few cautious steps forward. I ignored how we were holding hands now. There were more important things to worry about right now than hand holding, like eavesdropping. "I think he just asked her out."

"Not surprising. He's serious about her. He thinks she's lovely."

"Of course she is. I can't hear. Shh."

"Why are you shushing me? You spoke first!"

I slapped a hand over his mouth to silence him and could feel him smiling under my fingers. He obediently stayed quiet as we listened for Cindy's response to Ben's "proposal".

"Thank you, Ben," she said quietly, fiddling with the edges of her sleeves. "But I just got out of a relationship."

"Two whole months ago," I whispered, though I understood that wasn't long for most people.

"And I'm not ready for a relationship right now," she finished. "With anyone."

"I understand," Ben said, then I stopped listening. I turned to Axel with my jaw dropped.

I was glad Cindy was reacting logically to this, rather than giving into the first boy who asked her out like she did with Axel during prom, but—

"Now I'm conflicted," I whispered. "I think she made the right decision but after seeing them together for this long, I'm really starting to believe they're perfect for each other," I said, unsure of my own feelings. Axel and I stayed frozen in place, letting Ben and Cindy turn a corner and move out of sight.

"Perfect as in book perfect or just normal perfect?" Axel clarified, removing my hand from his lips.

"Normal perfect. Let's not bring up the book thing. It's irrelevant."

He grinned, liking the sound of that.

"I'm just shocked she didn't even tell him to wait or anything. It's clear she likes him back."

"She's just not ready, that's all. Don't worry. Ben's a gentleman. He won't push her."

"And that's good. I'm just..." I paused, staring up at the darkening pink sky. "Maybe I misread her. Maybe she was just being polite. Maybe she doesn't actually like him."

Axel shrugged.

Cindy was becoming her own person now, in part because of our differing experiences, and it was making me realize just how separate we'd become. We used to be like twins, always reading each other's minds. Now, that connection was gone. "She needs to get to know him better before she sorts out her feelings." I whispered.

"I don't think you should interfere," Axel said, cutting my thoughts short.

"You're right." I sighed. "I can't believe I almost slipped back into old habits. Thanks," I said, embarrassed. "I should leave her to it. She knows what she's doing...most of the time."

He smiled again, his eyes crinkling at the edges. "But that last part, about them spending more time together, can still come true," he said, then reached into his back pocket and pulled out his wallet. I watched as he removed four tickets from it, engraved with tiny Ferris wheels. "I just received these amusement park tickets and was planning to invite you and Cindy."

My eyes widened, then I studied him suspiciously. "I thought you wanted me to stay out of their relationship. Why are you encouraging it now?"

"I'm not encouraging it. This is a separate matter." He leaned closer, nearly trapping me against the wall behind me. "Besides, I was planning to ask you out regardless of what happened between those two."

"I'll tell Cindy about it," I said, conceding. "But she might say no."

"Fine with me. I'm used to rejection," he said, raising his hands in defeat before he even knew the verdict. "You've made me immune to it."

I gave him a look telling him to zip it, which made him laugh, then accepted the tickets. "Thank you, Axel. Really. If she says yes, I'd love to go."

"Wonderful." He squeezed my hand, then started forward again. "I'll walk you home. Text me when Cindy gives you an answer."

Chapter 41

I asked Cindy about Ben that night while we were splayed out on her bed with some snacks in hand, watching a romantic comedy on my laptop. The film was about a couple who kept missing each other for over ten years. I hated how relatable it felt.

I tried to ease into the topic of Ben slowly at first, but she saw the curiosity written all over my face and eventually asked the question so I couldn't stumble through anymore stunted sentences.

"You want to know what happened between me and Ben, right?" she said quietly, handing me the bowl of microwave popcorn.

"...Yes."

"Well, there's nothing to tell," she said quietly, once again showing how we'd become different people. We were no longer attached at the hip, which was a good thing in a way, but also sad.

"I overheard," I finally admitted. "Axel and I were right behind you when he asked you out."

"I know. I felt bad for saying no," she admitted slowly. "But I just—" She finished chewing her popcorn, deliberating. She always considered things carefully before speaking. "I don't think I'm ready for any kind of relationship, and it's not just because of Derek. I'm not sure how I feel about Ben either."

"Oh." I paused, waiting for her to continue, but she didn't. "I thought you liked him," I admitted quietly, unsure if I should bring up the amusement park now.

"I'm not sure," she admitted. "I'd like some time to think it through, and he agreed to wait for me just like Axel agreed to wait for you."

"He what?" Had Axel spilled the beans about our entire relationship, or the lack thereof, to Ben? Well, I suppose it was fair, since I unloaded all my own secrets on Cindy too, but still!

"Yes. Ben seems like a nice guy, but then again, I might not be the best judge of that," Cindy said, unaware that my outburst was directed at Axel, not Ben. "But that's why I have you here, right? To give me a second opinion. If Ben doesn't seem like a good guy, you'll tell me right away."

"Of course I would. That's why I'm here." And I wouldn't hold back this time.

But if Cindy was firm in her decision to wait, it might be best to bring up the invitation now so she could reject it outright. "Then, I'm not sure if you're ready to come with Axel and me to the amusement park next week. Ben would be coming too so I'm not sure—"

Cindy smirked. I had never seen her smirk before. "You and Axel? Is it going to be a date?"

"No!" I said immediately. "Don't give me that look! It was always meant to be a four-person hangout!"

Cindy giggled and I let her. I wouldn't lay into her like I would Axel. "I get it, I get it. And I'd love to go," she said.

"You would? Seriously?" I was shocked. She was better at adjusting to uncomfortable situations than me, apparently, though that was probably because she wanted to set me and Axel up.

"Of course! And I hope it'll end up better than the festival last time," Cindy said. The fact that she added that last part with zero regret or animosity in her voice told me she was truly starting to heal. That meant more to me than anything else that had happened this week.

"Now that we're on the subject of you and Axel," Cindy said slowly. "What are you—"

"Don't even start, you!"

Cindy giggled again, happier than she'd been since high school. "I'll ask *after* the date then."

"It's not a date!"

Chapter 42

The day of the amusement park trip arrived quickly, and I wasn't too happy about getting up before the sun did. It was going to be a long ride so we had to get an early start. At least we weren't like the boys, who accidentally booked tickets for even earlier bus and couldn't change them in time.

I boarded the bus with Cindy, outfitted in a simple pair of pants and a thin purple sweater just in case the weather got colder. As the bus took us outside the city and I settled in for a several-hour trip, I got the sense that this date might fully determine where my relationship with Axel stood. In the last week alone, my suspicions about him treating women differently were confirmed. Sure, one month wasn't enough time to see sustained changes, but my hopes were already rising and there was no stopping them now. I had been eagerly waiting for an excuse to follow my heart, rather than my head.

Plus, I got the feeling that if I rejected Axel again, technically for the third time, it would be the last. It was a well-known fact that three strikes took you out.

It took hours to reach the outskirts of Toronto where Canada's Wonderland rested, but once we arrived, it was a beautiful and harrowing sight. We could see the high tracks of several roller coasters rising above the buildings and bridges around us, as well as one of those tall towers that you could ride to the top of, then be dropped from without warning. I vowed to never get on that one.

Axel and Ben met us at the entrance, whining to us about having to wait an extra hour thanks to their own mistake.

Axel looked thrilled to see us. Meanwhile, Ben greeted Cindy with the same platonic smile he gave to everybody, and she only seemed slightly more nervous than usual due to the reaction. I tried not to worry about it. If Cindy was actually worried, she wouldn't have come in the first place.

We spent the first couple of hours going on the same rides, many of which had a thirty-to-forty-minute line. Thanks to the extreme wait times, we had to find ways to entertain ourselves. There were plenty of word games we came up with, then we switched to telling stories with silly punchlines, and finally concluded the wait with intensely competitive thumb wars. Most of them were between Axel and Ben, thankfully, since the hand holding aspect was bound to be a little...tense between two "not" couples who had rejected each other in the past.

The roller coasters were fun and made me feel like I was flying for a few brief moments, but the upside-down ones made my stomach flip in a way that made me want to vomit or pass out or both. Axel caught onto this quick and offered to sit the next upside-down ones out with me. He framed it as wanting to get something to eat but I knew that wasn't the real reason. Not only was he doing it for my sake but he was also afraid of the rides.

"To be honest," Axel lied as we stood in front of the roller coaster, watching Cindy and Ben wait in line. "I took a break from riding because I wanted to give those two a moment alone."

"I thought we weren't interfering."

"Hm?" He shot me an innocent look. "We're not. We're buying beaver tails. Have you had those before?"

I wrinkled my nose. "Sounds disgusting."

"Exactly." Axel's eyes sparkled as he led me away from the ride toward the food stands. His grin widened even more when I found out "beaver tails" were just flat, round pastries. He'd led me on with tales of gross beaver meat while we walked so the look of shock I had when I was handed something delicious-looking and sweet made him laugh. The treats were similar to churros but flat, soft, and coated in both cinnamon and sugar. Mine melted in my mouth.

We chatted about our grades while coming to rest on a bench with a good view of the ride Cindy and Ben were currently on, then we discussed the video game he'd bought, and finally a restaurant Axel wanted to try out.

"I was thinking of inviting you," he said quietly, doing that upturned look where his blue eyes studied me, searching for the answer before I said it aloud. "Just you and me, that is." Was that a bit of pink on the top of his cheeks? It was so rare to see him blush.

"I'm glad you brought that up." My stomach flip-flopped again, though it felt good this time. "Axel, about us. I may have had a change—"

Of course, just like in a dumb book, we were interrupted right as we were getting to the good part. Ben and Cindy had finished their ride and found us, ready to keep exploring. The moment between Axel and me was gone.

"I really want to try that one," Ben said, pointing out a slide with water at the bottom. It was meant to splash you at the end, though not so much that you needed a swimsuit. "It might not suit the weather right now, but I would love to try it anyway. It's one of the few rides I haven't been on yet, ever."

"Sure." I glanced at Axel, then paused. He looked a little paler than usual and his fists were clenched. He must be scared of the ride, or maybe it was the water. I couldn't be sure. If he was scared of both Ferris wheels and water rides, I wondered why he kept inviting us to places like this.

I looked at Cindy next, and she was fiddling with her belt. I could tell at a glance that she didn't want to ride it either.

"Do you two want to take a break?" I asked, "while Ben and I try that ride?"

Axel said yes immediately. "Thank you. Cindy? Do you want to grab a bite or go to the bathroom?"

Cindy nodded, looking ready to collapse from having to ride such an apparently frightening thing. "See you soon, Zilla."

"More like in half an hour." Ben nodded at the line. "If you two get lonely without us, you can join us in the line."

"I'd rather sit in the shade, thank you very much," Axel countered jokingly, then led Cindy away. I felt a pang of loneliness as soon as their backs were turned, but I brushed it off.

"So," Ben said as we joined the row of waiting people. "Tell me about you and Axel. He doesn't say much when I ask, so I figured it would be best to go to the source—as long as I'm not intruding or making you uncomfortable, that is."

I gulped and leaned against the railing locking us into the line. "As long as you tell me about you and Cindy," I countered, wanting to get a full read on him and his intentions. He'd stuck around this long, even after getting rejected, so I wanted to know why.

"Fair enough." We stepped forward a few more feet, then went back to waiting. "I think you already know why I like her. I can tell you identified all her great traits long before I did."

That sounded very clinical but I didn't mind. I was the same way during my book theory phase. "Such as?" I needed to hear him explain why he liked her. If the answer was something superficial or focused on what he could take from her, he would fail my test.

"Her kindness, first of all, though that's obvious. Her passion. She loves her hobbies and the people around her to death. I love seeing her eyes light up when she talks about you."

"You're not just trying to butter me up, are you?" I asked, raising an eyebrow and holding back a smile.

"No, not this time. If I ever date her, I'll be sure to do it, though. I know I'll need to get both your permission and her parents'."

I chuckled. "Fair. What else?"

He went on to list a few more traits: her eyes, her hard-working personality, her compassion for others, her love of games and shows, how she reacted fearfully at certain things but still stood up to them. I doubted that last part for a moment, but then I realized he was right. Cindy had developed a backbone and he had noticed it before I did. I had claimed she was still in the learning stage, but in Ben's eyes, she'd already reached the next level.

"So, do I pass?" he asked finally.

"For now." He certainly did. His tone seemed genuine too. "Now I suppose you want to hear back from me?"

"Yup." He flashed me a toothy grin.

"So, what do you want to know?"

"If you like him back."

That was blunt.

Well, no sense hiding it. "I do."

"But you're afraid, I take it? Axel didn't say it outright, but I got the feeling when I saw you two interact. To be frank, I don't blame you. I know how he acted a few years ago. I used to be the same way, so I won't sugarcoat it."

"But you changed?" I couldn't be sure I believed it.

"I'm trying. Sometimes I struggle. I get tempted to go back to how I was, but I believe following God's will for a long-lasting relationship will be worth it in the long run. I think Axel believes that too. He thinks *you're* worth it, Zilla."

There it was—that feeling of confirmation. Just like at the college party, where my love for Axel became real, I felt absolute elation knowing I'd finally be able to pursue Axel without fear. Well, the fear would still be there, but I was willing to face it like Cindy did. Axel was worth it. I wanted him and he wanted me. We would try to make it work. He was ready, so I could be too.

Ben and I had reached the front of the line now. The people ahead of us were climbing onto thick tubes, preparing to ride down a tunnel to the bottom of the slide. I noticed how soggy everyone's pant legs became when they emerged from the other end of the tunnel, but I didn't mind a little water. The sun was still beating down on us from its perch high in the sky and would dry our clothes quickly.

As I peered over the railing, I spotted Axel and Cindy. They were holding slushies now. His was blue and hers was pink. They also had a purple and orange one resting on the bench beside them, presumably for Ben and me.

Something was wrong, though.

My heart leapt into my throat, choking me for a second.

Axel had his arm wrapped around Cindy's shoulders, protectively, possessively. That wasn't a friendly hug. It was something he would have done to girls a month ago, before he tried to stop flirting.

Ben noticed my distress and looked down. His brow furrowed.

"What do you think they're doing?" I asked, not wanting to misunderstand the situation. I detested miscommunication tropes in books more than anything. Now it was happening to me.

Ben didn't respond, so I knew it looked just as bad as I thought.

This went against everything Ben had just said about Axel putting in effort to rid himself of his playboy ways. He hadn't changed at all!

But...wait...

My old habit of believing we were living inside a book returned for just a moment. I thought about Cindy and how her love story with Derek had fallen through. I'd read a few stories where the boy or girl started the story with someone who was wrong for them, then when that person was out of the picture, their real partner came along and gave them a happy ending. My favorite aspect of those stories was when the real soul mate was there from the very start, ignored by the protagonist until it was the right time.

Cindy had dated Derek at first, until he showed his true colors and left. Now Axel was here, and he'd been in the background the entire time, helping from the sidelines without interfering.

Now that Derek was gone, Axel could step in and finally be revealed as the true love interest. He *had* taken an interest in her when they first met, right?

What if—

What if the author's plan all along had been for those two to get together, and I'd just been a pawn, used to keep Axel present in the story? Or what if he hadn't come to Canada for me after all? What if he lied and actually came for Cindy?

My thoughts were running wild as the park instructor told me to climb into the vacant tube. I knew I was being irrational. I knew I was falling right into the miscommunication trope too. But I was angry. It felt like the universe was taunting me, telling me I was wrong to believe in Axel after all.

"Zilla!" Ben called to me as my tube started to move forward. "Be careful when you reach the bottom."

"Why?" Was the ride dangerous? It was weird that he brought it up now, right before I went down.

"There's some guy down there with Axel and Cindy," he answered. "He looks like the—"

Then I was speeding down the slide and couldn't hear him anymore. Typical. Yet another annoying book trope—missing the most crucial part of the statement. I couldn't even enjoy the tube ride since I was starting to panic about whatever dangerous person was waiting at the bottom for me. The water that had seemed exciting a moment ago turned out to be biting cold and frustrating. If someone was causing trouble for Cindy, they'd have to face a grumpy, drenched, pissed-off Godzilla now.

Chapter 43

Climbing out of the tube without slipping into the knee-deep water was difficult, even with the help of an attendant in red, but I managed it and was back on dry pavement in less than a minute. I immediately marched in the direction of Axel and Cindy's last location. I wasn't sure what was going on, but I'd drifted from dismayed at the sight of them practically hugging, to outright angry that something even worse might be going on. I wasn't sure which of those two emotions were worse.

I discovered the pair fairly quickly. They had moved away from their original position but were still out in the open. The tray of extra slushies had been placed on the pavement, forgotten. Once I was within earshot, I understood why.

"Zilla!" Cindy spotted me first and immediately pushed Axel away. It wasn't in an *"I got caught doing something I shouldn't have"* way, but rather an *"I want you to protect me instead"* way. There wasn't a look of guilt on Axel's face either, which made me wonder what kind of context I had missed to make them hug each other like that. I got the answer a moment later.

"I think I saw Derek," Cindy hissed as soon as she barreled into me, hugging me tight like a frightened child. "Axel shielded me from him so I wouldn't get discovered but when I looked again, he was gone."

"That can't be. He's in America. It must have been a look-a-like." It wasn't possible for Derek to be here, after getting arrested. Even if he wasn't put in prison, he still wouldn't be allowed to cross an international border anytime soon. Besides, even if he did return to Canada, how would he know we were here specifically in this amusement park? Unless we really were living in a book—

"I don't know how he got here but I know it was him," Cindy insisted. She had pulled me over to Axel by this point, then she pointed at a bathroom a few feet away. "I really need to go to the bathroom, but I didn't want to go in alone."

"And I don't feel like getting arrested for entering a girls' bath-room," Axel added. His tone was casual, but his face told me he was still jumpy from the encounter.

"Did you see Derek too?" I asked him. Cindy could have been mistaken but if Axel saw him too, it had to be real.

Axel's eyes were somber as he nodded. "It was him. I don't know how he got here."

It's a book! We're living in a book! I was right all along! The author wants more drama. That has to be it. That's why she brought him back despite it making zero sense!

I silenced the irrational part of my brain and pulled a canister of pepper spray from my purse. "Take this, Cindy. If he shows up—" I demonstrated how to use it. "Spray him with this."

"What if it doesn't stop him?"

"Use it, then run. Should we call the police too?" I directed the question at Axel, who looked unsure.

"I'm not sure if they're allowed to arrest him just for showing up."

"What's going on here?"

Our conversation was interrupted when a loud voice broke through. I jumped, as did Cindy and Axel, but we all relaxed when Ben joined us, soaked from the tube ride. He had already zeroed in on the slushies and handed me the purple one.

"Cindy's ex-boyfriend might be here," I whispered, then turned back to Axel and Cindy. "I think we should at least tell security—if they even have security here. Let's do it together, though, after we go to the bathroom."

Cindy nodded, eager for the help. She may have gotten braver over the past month, but it was easy to act brave when the threat wasn't present. Now the real test was here.

"Stay safe," I told Axel as I led Cindy to the bathroom. I didn't want him placing himself in danger again.

"I'll watch out for you," Axel said. He nodded at Cindy, but his eyes lingered on mine just a second longer.

My mind was whirring as I led Cindy into the smelly bathroom. I stayed right by the front door, guarding it vigilantly, but I also kept a clear view of the stalls. I doubted Derek would sneak in here beforehand to get the drop on us but if this was a book—

No! I swore I would give up on the book idea—

But it was the only thing that made sense right now.

Cindy was flushing the toilet when I heard a commotion outside. It consisted of two male voices yelling at each other.

I strained to listen. One of those voices belonged to Axel. The other—

"She's not here and even if she was," Axel was saying roughly, "you shouldn't be here at all, Derek! Do you want to get arrested again?"

When I heard his voice, a shiver ran down my spine. It was Derek all right, yet he shouldn't be here. This all felt so unnatural. How did he know to be here? Had he been stalking us all month? That felt impossible.

"I don't want to hear that from a bastard like you," Derek said, then he laid out a few more curse words to describe Axel adequately.

"How did you even know I was here?" Axel asked, carefully leaving out the word "we" so Derek wouldn't know Cindy and I were here too.

"I..." Derek paused, as though thinking up a reason. Once again, my stomach flip-flopped as I wondered whether Derek got here himself, or if the author had pulled some strings to get him here. "I put a tracker on Cindy's phone!" he said finally, but it sounded like he'd been searching for any explanation that made sense and just shouted the first thing that came to mind. His voice was tinged with a hint of triumph at his answer, like he was pleased with his clever lie.

Axel paused. Maybe he was thinking the same thing. Derek's appearance felt too convenient, too strange.

"I'm going to call security if you don't beat it," Axel threatened.

"I can still break that nose of yours before they reach us," Derek threatened in return, and I could tell he meant it. "Always chasing after Cindy, even when she was dating me. You had to have known this was coming."

I glanced back at Cindy's stall, silently begging her to come out. I had to help Axel.

Derek was loudly recounting all the times Axel had flirted with Cindy, using it as an excuse to get back at him. Yet nearly all those incidents had been my fault, not Axel's! I'd asked him to do it to hurry the romance plot along! I should be the one getting a broken nose, not Axel! Wait, no, that was stupid. No one should be getting a broken nose!

I started scouring the bathroom for something I could use as a weapon, then jumped when I heard a shout from some lady outside, reacting to something Derek had just done. He must have struck the first blow. Then I heard Ben begging Derek to stop before someone got hurt. Sadly, that was exactly what Derek wanted.

"Everyone treats me like the bad guy," Derek shouted, then I heard a punch land. I hoped it wasn't on Axel's face. "But you're the one who took advantage of people, Axel! You're the one hurting people. I'm trying to stop jerks like you from ruining sweet girls like Cindy!"

"Cindy," I hissed. We had to act now!

Derek swung again and I heard another thud.

Cindy finally stepped out of the stall, but she was shaking. She must have heard everything and wasn't in the right mind to help. It probably took all her courage just to exit the stall.

She wouldn't join in on the fight and I didn't expect her to. No one should have to enter such a dangerous situation. Besides, I was the one who got us into this mess, so I should be the one to take care of it.

"Stay here," I told her, clenching my fists. "Derek's out there but he doesn't know you're here. I'll try to stop him." I might end up punching him myself. "If things go south, run away and hide in a shop or something. Tell the shopkeeper to call security."

I didn't wait for Cindy to respond before dashing out of the bathroom. As soon as I swung around the entrance and into the open air, I caught a glimpse of the raging battle.

The people who had been walking past or relaxing on the nearby shaded benches were now slowly backing away from the two men brawling in the middle of the walkway.

It was definitely Derek, in the flesh and back from the US. He looked just as he had before but his face held a few new cuts and wrinkles. The scowl on his face looked like a permanent fixture, taking away the beguiling cuteness he used to possess. His Golden Retriever appearance wouldn't fool anyone anymore.

Derek was in a defensive stance, bouncing on the balls of his feet. Then, cursing, he stepped forward and punched Axel in the cheek again. Axel didn't fight back. If this had been a fair fight, he could have easily avoided the attacks, but as it was, I could see that he had placed himself strategically so Derek couldn't see the bathroom where Cindy and I were hiding.

I cringed as a trail of blood ran down the side of Axel's right eye. Hot, boiling rage filled my chest.

Derek swung again and Axel dodged this time, but he refused to run away because doing so would leave Derek free to hunt for me and Cindy.

Ben had run off, though not out of cowardice. He was speaking to the owner of a nearby pretzel shop. The shopkeeper was on the phone, presumably calling security. Good. Now I wouldn't have to do it.

I couldn't bear to see Derek punch the man I loved, so I chose to intervene, but I had to do so in a way that wouldn't jeopardize Cindy's safety. Maybe I could taunt him, leading him away from the bathroom so Cindy could make a break for it.

That seemed risky, though. Then again, punching him didn't seem smart either. I wasn't strong, especially compared to him.

Either way, the fact that I desperately wanted to punch him remained. It would probably hurt my fist more than his face, but it would feel satisfying for that one second. Plus, that was what stereotypical, best friend characters did. They punched the jerk who hurt the main character. Just once more, I wanted to play into that stereotype. Maybe it would appease the author, whose presence I was beginning to believe in again.

Then, after I punched him, I'd subvert the clichés and run away, hopefully with Axel in hand.

It was a stupid plan, but this whole situation was stupid, so it kind of called for it.

"Stand still," Derek growled, trying and failing to hit Axel again. The closer I got, the more cuts and forming bruises I could see on Axel's face. Derek planned to break Axel's nose by the end of this fight, if not more. He really was lucky Axel wasn't fighting back or running away.

"Derek!" I shouted, knowing I'd regret drawing his attention but I needed him to turn and face me so I could land a hit. Then I'd run and hope he chased me...Sure, he was faster but maybe that would give Axel an opening to escape.

Oh, this was all such an awful idea.

Derek turned to me and I pulled my fist back, swinging before I could change my mind. The look of surprise on his face was overshadowed by the searing pain in my knuckles as soon as my hand made contact with his cheek. I could feel his cheekbone under my knuckles, and it felt much stronger than my finger bones did.

Derek stumbled back but I did too, groaning and clutching my stinging knuckles. They were already going numb from the impact.

"Xiang!" Axel shouted, grabbing Derek from behind and pulling him away from me. "What are you doing? Get out of here!"

I was about to do just that. I wasn't going to fall for the "standing around like an idiot" tactic or the "believing I could fight back when I had never fought before in my life" trope. I wasn't a fighter and never planned to be. I'd landed my one painful (for me) punch and was satisfied. Time to flee and draw Derek away until security arrived.

"You should run too!" I shouted back at Axel, then turned to escape.

Before my plan could succeed, Derek shoved Axel against the tree, hitting his head against the bark. I gasped as Axel slumped against the trunk.

Once Derek was free, he grabbed me by the back of my shirt, yanking me closer to him. I should have run instead of hesitating!

My own collar wrapped tightly around my throat as he yanked on it, strangling me, then I felt myself falling backwards onto the pavement. I closed my eyes and covered the back of my head with my hands as I braced for impact. The pavement scraped by fingers and gave me a jolt, my brain feeling like it was jostling around in my skull, but I survived and was able to open my eyes and look up.

Derek was raising his foot above me, right over my head. Judging by the sneer on his face, he planned to at least break my nose and then move onto even more vulnerable parts of my body.

His eyes were wide, filled with a mad frenzy I only ever saw in films. He almost looked possessed.

How had I ever thought this guy was a protagonist? He was a villain, through and through.

As we stared at each other, I imagined seeing the author's own eyes through Derek's, and I almost felt sorry for the guy. He was just a puppet on a string, like I used to be. The author was the real villain here and I would hate to die at the hands of some writer I'd never truly met.

Chapter 44

I gasped, first in surprise then relief, when Axel hit Derek in the head with a branch from the tree he'd been thrown against. It knocked Derek onto his knees and kept my head from getting crushed under his boot.

As I scrambled to my feet, I saw Derek lunge at Axel again, but this time more ferociously and with the intent to kill. He punched Axel straight in the nose, accentuated by a resounding crack, then wrapped his hands around Axel's throat while shoving him against the tree again so he couldn't pull away from the strangulation.

I looked for the stick Axel had just used as a weapon, but it had been tossed aside and was now sitting near some people watching from afar but not within arm's reach. The crowd, mostly women and children, were keeping a safe distance.

Ben was running back in our direction, but he wasn't going to make it in time to help Axel.

There were no other options. It had to be me. I had to be the one to act! This wasn't just a stupid brawl anymore. Axel would die if I didn't do something.

I stepped forward, Axel's choking gasps ripping my heart open, but then someone ran past me from behind, charging right at Derek. It happened so fast that I didn't realize the runner was

Cindy until she had already reached her ex and hit him in the back with her fist.

"Derek!" she shouted, her high voice standing out against the chokes of Axel and angry grunts of Derek.

Derek paused, stiffened at the sound of Cindy's voice, then slowly turned toward her, keeping his hands on Axel's throat but loosening his grip. He couldn't have expected Cindy to face him head-on like this.

For a moment, I was afraid Cindy would try to punch him again. She was even weaker than me. Doing that would only anger Derek more, if that was even possible. I was already imagining him slapping her across the face, making her fall and smash her head open on the pavement.

I took another step forward to help, opening my mouth to scream a warning, but Cindy acted first. She raised her other hand, which was holding a black cannister, then pressed the top of it.

It was the pepper spray I gave her.

My eyes widened as a red-orange liquid shot out of the can directly into Derek's eyes. He screamed, releasing Axel's chokehold so he could block the spray with his palms, but Cindy had already hit his eyes and mouth.

As he shrieked in agony and swung his arms toward her, she stepped back so he couldn't knock her over.

Axel leapt away from Derek, then ran to me and pulled me back to safety. He was coughing and gasping, bruises already forming around his throat and under his eyes, but he still prioritized me over the lack of air entering his lungs.

A second later—as Derek fell to his knees once again and started rubbing the sleeves of his shirt all over his teary eyes and stinging mouth—Ben finally reached Cindy and pulled her back too. She was still standing in front of Derek, spray can at the ready for a second round, and her feet were spread apart confidently. Cindy wasn't a damsel in distress for me to save anymore. She was ready to stand up to her ex, even if her legs were still shaking as she did it.

My chest swelled with pride.

Derek wasn't even close to recovering from the pain when two security guards arrived and led him away, hopefully for good this time. As his feet dragged on the ground, I heard him shout through his tears, sending up one final plea to us and the universe:

"I never should have met you, Cindy! I was a nice person until you came along! I was normal before I met you! You have no idea—" Then he went out of earshot.

My grip on Axel's bloodied hands tightened as we listened to his desperate cries.

Had I been right about the possession? It truly sounded like he was being controlled by something or someone. That, or he had experienced such an abrupt personality shift that it had driven him crazy.

Again, if we truly were living in a book, there was a small chance Derek had started off as a normal, well-rounded person and was later turned into a monster by the author to add suspense and tension to an otherwise peaceful story. If that truly was the case, I felt sorry for him. No one deserved that.

My chest tightened at the thought that Derek might truly come to believe he was evil. If this was the author's doing, he needed to know. If I explained everything, maybe there was a chance for him to come back from all this, to return to the normal person he used to be before he became a male lead turned antagonist.

"I'll be right back," I said to the others, avoiding telling Axel what I planned to do. I wasn't sure how he'd react to my admittance that I was going to comfort the guy who had just beaten him up. "Stay here."

They all nodded but Axel watched, confused, as I ran after Derek. He didn't stop me, though. He trusted me and my judgement...most of the time.

Derek was still shouting at the top of his lungs when I caught up, but his voice had quieted, and it sounded like he was choking on his own words. The spray must have gotten into his throat.

"This isn't me," he sobbed, struggling to stand as tears streamed from his red eyes. "It's not."

"Wait." I stopped a few feet away from him, not wanting to risk another punch, and the guards glanced at me questioningly. "I just want to tell him something," I told them.

The guards shared a look, then shrugged. "Sure?"

Derek was staring at me, panting heavily from all the adrenaline and tears. He truly looked pitiful, with red streaks staining his cheeks and bruises forming on both sides of his face.

"Derek, I heard what you said," I began, aware of how obvious that was and how dumb I sounded. But this might be my only chance to speak to him again. If I didn't say this now, I'd regret it later.

"I..." How could I even put this into words without sounding like a moron? "I understand how you feel. You feel like you're being controlled."

The slight glimmer in his eyes told me it was true. He knew I was being genuine and that I understood exactly what he meant. We really were just puppets on strings, acting in someone else's play.

"You might feel like we've been placed into archetypes by someone and you can't escape the role you've been given," I continued, "The role of a villain."

He didn't say anything so I kept going.

"But I know it's not true. We *can* escape those paths we've been forced down. Just because we've been given a role doesn't mean we have to follow it. I've seen all of us break out of our archetypes—me, Cindy, Axel."

I'd heard authors occasionally say they felt like they 'lost control of their characters' or that the characters had a mind of their own. I had to believe it was true.

"Axel isn't a playboy anymore." Or a rival who solely existed for jealous drama. "Cindy's no longer defenseless." Or a damsel in need of saving. "And I'm no longer the person you knew before." The sassy BFF whose only role was to watch over Cindy. "I know you can change. Cindy's moved on, so it's time for you to do it too. I believe you when you say you used to be a good person. You can be that person again." And if I said it out loud, if there really was an author watching us from above, hopefully she'd take this dialogue as a sign that it was time to let Derek go.

Both of the guards were looking at me like I'd lost my mind and should be dragged alongside Derek to wherever they were going, but I could tell Derek agreed with me.

"Maybe I will," he said quietly.

I believed him.

"Thanks," he muttered before walking away, leaving our lives for good. Watching him exit the stage made me feel like I'd truly brought an end to this author's rule over us. We were free to make our own decisions now. Maybe we always had been. I couldn't be sure and never would be.

Regardless, I was glad I had spoken to him. I hoped he could return to the way he claimed he was before. Without the author's interference, maybe he could turn into the sweet boy we all initially thought he was.

None of my friends asked what I had done when I returned to them, but I could tell both Axel and Cindy had a good guess.

"You know," Axel whispered in my ear, leaning his chin against my shoulder as I rejoined him, "Listening to him talk, I started to believe all your theories about us living inside a book."

I chuckled, wiping a tear from my eye as the adrenaline from the fight faded. "Me too."

"Let's hope he gets some professional help," Ben said as he and Cindy approached us, shaken but smiling. "I thought you said he was sent to the United States. How did he find us here?"

I shrugged, no longer caring if his appearance was a coincidence, contrived, or had a real explanation. Regardless, we were all safe and this time there was no question that Derek would now be charged and sent to prison. While there hadn't been enough evidence to prove he'd had been trying to abduct Cindy previously, this latest incident would certainly change things and Cindy would finally be free of him for good.

I glanced over my shoulder at Axel and studied his face, intensely relieved that he was okay. If he had been killed, it would have broken a part of me that I'd just recently unearthed. Losing him would feel like losing a part of myself now.

"Should we take you two to the hospital?" Ben asked, looking both of us over. "Or," he continued, gesturing toward the Ferris wheel, "do you want to end the night on a *high* note?" He raised an eyebrow, then took a moment to laugh at his own pun. Cindy seemed to find it funny and offered a polite laugh, but I rolled my eyes. This wasn't the time for lame puns, even if I appreciated the attempt.

"I'll look us over first," I said, eager to put my nursing skills to use. "Then we'll see. Axel's afraid of heights anyway. You didn't know that, Ben?" They were best friends, after all.

When Ben grinned sheepishly, I realized he *did* know and just wanted to tease Axel about it.

Axel didn't respond when I pointed to a bench we could sit on. He had been resting his head on my shoulder throughout our entire conversation and for a second, I worried he'd passed out, had a concussion, or had fallen asleep from exhaustion, but then he raised his head and spoke. "Sure. Look me over, then we'll go up." He didn't look too pleased about boarding the Ferris wheel.

I did a thorough check and was able to rule out any issues that would need immediate attention, but Axel and I agreed to visit a walk-in clinic once we returned to Ottawa, just to be safe. The crack I'd heard and assumed was his nose being broken must have come from Derek's knuckles instead.

As we exited the scene of the climax, I made a note to never return to this amusement park again.

Chapter 45

Our final ride on the Ferris wheel got delayed when a third security guard showed up to make a report on the incident. He didn't ask us to come back with him or speak to the police, but we did have to give him our phone numbers and promise to answer right away if he called. I was sure we'd have to recount everything in detail to the police later, but since the guard left after he got what he needed from us, I tried not to dwell on it for the moment.

Once we were alone again, we joined the line in front of the massive ferris wheel and stared at the small cars full of people as they rose above our heads. They only swung occasionally, but I felt Axel's grip on my hand tighten every time they tipped.

"You can just say no," I whispered in his ear to reassure him, but he shook his head.

"If this is a book," he said in an equally hushed tone, "Then I don't want to anger the author by refusing to follow the cliché. She might send Derek back to us as punishment."

My jaw dropped, though I did it for dramatic effect rather than as a genuine reaction. "I thought you told me I shouldn't believe in that type of stuff."

"Well...I'll only believe it for one day," Axel said, shrugging it off. "And tomorrow, we'll return to normal. I don't want it dictating your every move, after all."

"Right." For once, I felt like someone was truly understanding me and it felt good. The fact that it was Axel made it even better. He'd criticized the idea for a whole year.

The wait to board the ride was only twenty minutes, but that gave me plenty of time to think about my future relationship with Axel and what I planned to do with him from now on.

I now understood why I'd seen Axel and Cindy hugging below the tube ride—he'd been hiding her from Derek. However, that feeling of possession over Axel had been real regardless, hinting at my true emotions bubbling under the surface.

I didn't want to sit on the sidelines anymore, leading Axel on and refusing to choose a side. It was time to tell him how I felt. I planned to do it during the ride—it would be our one chance to be alone today—and if I waited until tomorrow, I might be able to talk myself out of it, so I had to act now.

Axel looked blissfully unaware of the mountain of emotions rising in me as we moved down the line, but he was probably still thinking about being strangled, so I didn't blame him for not noticing.

"You two go ahead," Ben said when we reached the front of the line. "I'll keep an eye out for Derek until you get back," he added quietly so Cindy couldn't hear. "But with that pepper spray, I doubt she'd need my help anyway."

I grinned at Cindy when he said that, noticing how she still kept the can in the top of her purse. That was the first time anyone had said such a thing about her. It made me feel like a mother watching her child finally grow up.

"See you in a few minutes," I said, emphasizing the 'few' for Axel's sake. Making the trip into the air sound short might lessen his anxiety.

Then we climbed into the metal, wobbly box and sat across from each other.

I turned to wave at Cindy and Ben while Axel gripped both sides of his seat. He was muttering under his breath about being trapped inside a cage, then he squeaked when there was a sudden jerk. I kept quiet as he paled. I was waiting for the perfect moment to confess my feelings, and this wasn't it.

As the people below us got smaller, resembling ants, I got a gorgeous view of the rides around us (and a not so gorgeous view of the suburbs surrounding the park). Then I glanced at Axel again. Sadly, he still wasn't in a position to hear my feelings. He was gripping the handles even tighter than before and biting his lip. When the small box we were in moved slightly to the side, halfway around the giant loop, he groaned.

"I'm sorry, Zilla, but I think I'm gonna sit on the floor," he whispered, then did just that. "After getting punched in the face and now this, I can't pretend to be composed," he admitted, his voice adorably wobbly and full of shame for looking weak in front of me.

"It's okay," I said, suppressing a giggle and taking a seat beside him. His one hand was still gripping the seat, but I took his other hand in mine, giving it a comforting squeeze.

"Distract me," he ordered, studying our surroundings with heavy breaths. "Tell me something that will disgust me."

"Disgust you?" Well, now I couldn't confess. If that disgusted him, I doubted we could go through with it.

A smirk rising across my face, I realized what I had to do. If he wanted a distraction, I'd give him one.

Releasing his hand, I grabbed the front of his shirt and pulled him closer. He turned to look at me, finally, and confusion covered his face. He had no clue what I was about to do.

The kiss I gave him was about as awkward as the drunken one in the university, though we had switched roles this time. Now *he* was the one in shock and I was the one making the move.

I pressed our lips together and enjoyed feeling him go from frightened—not of me but of the ride, thank goodness—to relaxed, then a little excited. By the time we pulled apart, just as I'd intended, he was completely distracted from his fear of heights.

We stared at each other for a few seconds, breathing heavily and feeling our hearts pound in unison. Then he made a show of clearing his throat before speaking.

"I suppose that's one way to do it," he said quietly, a blush creeping across his cheeks before he composed himself. "Can I take this to mean you're...not against being with me like you were before?"

I lowered my head, turning shy now that the moment was over, then nodded. "Ben told me about your effort to change and I've seen it in action."

"I didn't think you noticed," he said in response. "Took me long enough, I suppose."

"Yeah." A weight lifted off my shoulders as he finally let his feelings show on his face again.

His eyes had specks of gold among the blue. I'd never seen them this close before, at least not for a while. They were pretty.

"I love you," he whispered, his voice husky, and I was finally able to say it back with confidence.

"I love you too."

"Even though I was the love rival in your best friend's story?"

I gave a pretend huff. "I thought we weren't supposed to discuss that anymore."

"Yeah, well, like I said, Derek's appearance may have enlightened me—"

"You were the biggest advocate against it!"

"And I still am, because of how it was changing your world view. But now you don't let it control you, so it's fine for me to start considering it—"

We'd just kissed and now we were back to bickering again.

I was happy to finally feel validated when it came to my wacky worldview, but I could tell Axel was teasing me rather than actually considering the theory, so I allowed myself to act a little outraged. It was obvious he didn't mind our arguments as long as they were all in good fun. "We've finally made our relationship official and we're already fighting," I warned him.

"Then should I kiss you again?" he asked, his wide grin revealing teeth so bright they nearly reflected the light shining through the Ferris wheel windows.

I didn't answer, crossing my arms indignantly. There was no point speaking anyway, since he was already leaning in for that second kiss. I was sure there'd be many more to come.

I couldn't help smiling as he pulled me closer, not showing the slightest fear as the Ferris wheel cage wobbled again.

So, it finally happened. After nearly two and a half years, the girl who had been type cast as the single best friend had finally received her happy ending. Despite absolutely hating the idea of being roped into a romance with the stereotypical playboy, I was pretty happy with how things turned out.

I'd always rolled my eyes at the line: "Everyone is the main character of their own story" but after everything I'd experienced in the last two years, I realized I hadn't given that notion enough credit. I always figured the quote was an attempt to make people feel better about themselves and their dreary lives, but now I was starting to believe it.

Epilogue

y high school and university graduations could not have been more different.

The second one had a lot more debt tacked onto it, of course, but I didn't mind that part. I'd earned enough scholarships to get by.

No, what really mattered was who sat in the audience and beside me as I waited to receive my expensive slip of paper. During high school, it was just me and Axel, acknowledging that our parents weren't there while stuffing ourselves at a buffet.

This time, things were different.

As I crossed the auditorium's stage to receive my degree from a faculty member I'd never met—I didn't even know his official title—I heard claps and cheers from a few people behind me. Some of the girls who had shared nursing classes with me and had become study buddies during that time, cheered as I marched forward. The students in other majors—like Cindy, Axel, and lots of friends from the club—cheered from the front rows where they were waiting to be called.

As I was handed a rolled-up piece of paper I'd spent thousands of dollars on, I shook the mystery man's hand and turned toward the audience. I met Axel's eyes first, my fiancé. He looked just as he did before, only with a few new smile lines already forming around his eyes. Next I looked for Cindy, who was smiling and clapping harder than everyone else. Her cheeks were bright red from the excitement.

Then, I finally found them further back in the crowd—my parents. My mother wasn't smiling but she looked proud. Her arms were crossed over her teal dress and her strawberry-blonde hair was pulled up in a tight bun. The serious expression on her face had been passed onto me, but I could see the beginning of a smirk forming. It was what happened when she wanted to smile but was staying composed. She was happy to see me graduate but was probably feeling bad that she had missed so many of the important moments in my life that got me here.

My father, on the other hand, looked like Cindy. He was clapping so hard his hands would definitely hurt after this and his grin was as wide as Axel's, if not wider.

My brother Hyson was seated next to him, looking nearly identical to our father but shorter and with a wrinkled dress shirt and tie tucked into his pocket. Hyson was at that age when he didn't want to smile because that wasn't cool, but he was present all the same and that was what mattered to me.

Today would be the first time my family officially met Axel and Axel had been moaning about it all day, worried he'd leave a poor first impression. I had assured him plenty of times that my father wasn't hard to please, but it was my mother who had him nervous. She would be the tougher egg to crack. Regardless of how the meeting went, though, Axel would be joining us on our family trip to China next month so I was sure it would give him plenty of time to charm and impress my mother.

Degree in hand and the posing for pictures completed, I headed off the stage and took my seat amongst my fellow future nurses. My heart had never felt so full. The high school girl who had graduated four years ago, moping about having no friends, would be so pleased to see the turnout and hear all the cheers. I wasn't a big fan of cheering and screaming in general, but just for today, I'd allow it.

As the next group of students were called up, I turned around to see who else was sitting inside the giant gym, which had been converted into a stage for the ceremony. I could see Ben near the back, hands already poised to clap. He'd come for all our sakes, but we all knew his main reason for attending the ceremony was to cheer on his girlfriend, Cindy. The two had finally started dating a few months ago and I couldn't be more relieved. Cindy's nervous, shy, blushing personality had finally returned when she realized her feelings for Ben went beyond friendship, but I didn't have to worry about Ben becoming a creep. I knew him well enough to trust him fully with my best friend's future.

I was about to turn back, satisfied, when I thought I spotted another familiar face at the back of the building. I looked again and stifled a gasp. It was Derek.

I frowned and squinted, staying low so he wouldn't catch me staring.

He was standing by the door and looking toward Cindy. My gut reaction was to call security, but the look on his face gave me pause. The malice and defensive stance he used to have was gone. He instead looked sad, like a man regretting his previous actions and making the moves to change, just like Axel had done three years ago.

I saw the same look on Derek's face that Axel occasionally wore when he was tempted to revert back to his old self. We'd gone through couple's counseling together to help, and he was being held accountable by everyone, including me and Ben, so I was no longer worried like I used to be. But Derek, on the other hand, was a loose cannon. I had no way of knowing if he'd reverted back to the sweet boy who existed before the author molded him into her villain.

After a minute of discreetly watching him, nothing happened. He didn't make a move. He even stopped staring at Cindy after a while, focusing instead on the floor.

Deciding Derek didn't have ill intentions after all and had just come to see the graduation of his lost love, I turned back around and faced the front. I texted Axel about it though, just in case. I wouldn't tell Cindy. She'd already moved on. Hopefully this would give Derek the chance to as well.

The graduation wrapped up with a feeling of completion. If we really were living in a book, I got the sense it would end here.

There had been a bit of drama with our relationships over the last three years, but none of it had been worth writing home about and everything had settled down into the somewhat boring, comfortable life that came with long-term relationships and marriage. The coincidences had died down. This was the closest the author would ever get to a happy ending. I desperately hoped our story, if it was a real book, didn't sell well. Then the author could leave us alone and not milk it by turning our lives into a series. We didn't deserve that interference.

As soon as the ceremony ended, I got up from my seat and hurried toward Axel and Cindy, eager to bring them to my parents for the big introduction.

As I rushed to join them, I allowed myself to smile and give up on the romance novel mentality for real this time. Everyone else had moved on. It was time for me to do it too.

We'd had our happy ending.

Now it was time to start a new story, one that was just a little more boring and predictable, but just as steady and full of growth.

Other books by Jaysee Jewel

About the Author

Jaysee writes adult fantasy and horror (with the occasional dip into romance and soft science fiction).

She spends her free time reading, writing, playing video games, watching movies or anime, and playing with her cat.

If you're interested in seeing her upcoming releases or want to receive updates, you can visit her website at https://jayseejewel. mystrikingly.com/